The
Road to States

By
Mary Marino

Copyright © 2012 by Mary Marino

ISBN 978-0-7414-8179-5

Printed in the United States of America

This is a work of fiction. Names, characters, places, and incidents either are the product of the author's imagination or are used fictitiously. Any resemblance to actual events or locales or persons, living or dead, is entirely coincidental.

Published November 2012

INFINITY PUBLISHING
1094 New DeHaven Street, Suite 100
West Conshohocken, PA 19428-2713
Toll-free (877) BUY BOOK
Local Phone (610) 941-9999
Fax (610) 941-9959
Info@buybooksontheweb.com
www.buybooksontheweb.com

To athletes everywhere,

who give words to their dreams,

and then commit them to action.

Preface

We're going to be state champions, words easy enough to say. Most times it's just talk, a bunch of noise sent into the air. A player has to hold onto those words, a team must become connected by them, everyone concentrating everyday on catching and passing them back and forth like a bunch of jugglers, or else the words just fall to the ground. At least that's the way I see it.

(1)

Drumming my fingers on the dining hall table, I was oblivious to my teammates seated around me. It was still summer and the season hadn't even begun, but I was lost once again in my season-ending fantasy. It was always the same. My friend, Jules, and I would hoist the championship trophy high in the air for all our fans to see. My grip would be so tight my fingers would stick to the cold, hard metal, yet I wouldn't care. I'd never want to let it go 'cause having it in our possession would mean one thing. We'd be the top high school field hockey team in the state.

How many other girls hungered for the same thing? I didn't know, but one thing was sure, it would be what I would wish for when I blew out the candles on my birthday cake the next day, and if I could make two wishes the second would be …

I felt a poke in my ribs. "Hey Jackie, quit your daydreaming. She just called your name," my teammate, Lindsay Sayers, whispered, and then pointed to the hockey camp director standing in front of the university dining hall.

I glanced up. The woman had been reading out a list of players chosen for the campers versus coaches all-star game when my mind had zoned out and had gone into 'wish mode.'

"Jules Hanson," the woman called out next. Jules, who was sitting across from me, gave me a thumbs up sign as her identical twin, Tori, slapped her on the shoulder.

Warming up for the camp all-star game an hour later I could feel the flutters beginning in my stomach, the same ones I get before every game. These seemed to grow bigger with each passing moment 'cause I wasn't surrounded by my teammates all dressed in Northfield High's familiar blue and white. Instead I was wearing a red scrimmage vest, and except for Jules, I would be playing with a bunch of strangers and we wouldn't be facing other high school players either. Our opponents were the college athletes who had coached at the camp, as well as two or three of the foreign coaches. *What if I sucked?*

I missed a ball that Jules had hit to me, and as I went to retrieve it from under the bleachers, Jules jogged over to me. "Come on. We're ready. Let's get a drink before we start."

I followed her long, determined strides across the field — tap, tap, tapping the ball as I went. Jules looked over her shoulder. "Relax. We're going to show them what players from Northfield are all about."

That was Jules, always confident. But she was right. I needed to ditch the nerves. How could I expect to play for a state title if I couldn't face a simple camp all-star game? I caught up to Jules and gave her a belated fist bump, and after the all-star team gave a customary pre-game cheer, I jogged onto the field itching for the game to start.

The first few minutes were action-packed, all the campers sitting in the stands totally into it, oohing and aahing the great passing combinations and awesome stick moves of both teams. I was pumped. Then the unthinkable happened.

I took a shot on goal and the other team's goalie made a solid kick, clearing the ball away from the goal cage. Two opposing players pursued the loose ball, neither player slowing down as they approached their objective. It was like watching a catastrophe in slow motion, and when they hit, it was my friend Jules who was crumbling underneath the powerful Dutch player.

Hitting the ground, Jules yelled out as her ankle twisted against the Dutch player's stick. I watched the camp trainer and Tori rush out to Jules who was rolling on the ground clutching her leg. I was stunned. Jules always seemed so indestructible to me. Tall and fit from hours spent in the gym, it had always been other players that had gotten the worst of it if they even dared to bump into Jules. More importantly, Jules was a captain and Northfield's star defender. We needed her if we were going to do anything this year.

This can't be happening. Jules, get up. When she didn't, I finally woke from the nightmare in front of me and began to make my way across the field to my fallen friend. I picked up Jules' stick and tried my best to console her as Tori and some of the other players helped her to the sidelines.

Eventually the game continued on, but it wasn't the same without my friend on the field. I don't even remember who won. I only knew I'd had enough of camp. It was time to go home.

My brother, Matt, and his college roommate, Cooker, picked up the twins and me later that afternoon, and after we dropped off the crutches Jules had borrowed from the health center, we began the long five hour trip home from Virginia to New Jersey. As we left the heart of the university's colonial campus I finally settled in, sandwiched in the back seat between my two best friends. Jules was staring out the window, her left leg stretched out over mine, a bag of ice resting on her injured ankle. Tori, on the other side of me, had her arm resting across the back of the seat. It had been like this, all of us intertwined, ever since the twins had moved to town during fifth grade.

For awhile I was feeling content returning home from such a successful time spent in camp, but then Tori started leaning forward in the space between Matt and Cooker wrapping herself up in their college stories, and Jules pulled out her cell and dialed Kate Carson, our other captain. A few miles more and I began to sense that something was off, like I was in the back seat all by myself. I studied the twins for a few moments and decided that maybe I was being a little oversensitive and just needed to catch up on my sleep.

I woke when we arrived at the twins' house, Jules inching my head off her shoulder as she tried to exit the car. Her dad was waiting in the driveway anxious to get her to the hospital for X-rays of her foot. Tori did a quick run into the house for a change of clothes. She was staying overnight at my house to help celebrate my birthday the next day. I wished Jules was coming too, but I think the ankle nixed that idea.

(2)

The next morning the bedroom door slowly squeaked open and my little sister, Lizzie, flew across the room yelling "Happy Birthday," then dove on top of me.

Oof! I wasn't prepared for how solid her body had become and it dawned on me the baby of our family was quickly growing up. How had I missed it? Was I that busy with hockey this summer?

"Oh no, is this how it feels to be so old?" I moaned squirming beneath her. "Maybe I shouldn't be having another birthday." I flipped her off my back, and found a favorite tickle spot under her chin.

She pushed my hands away. "Aren't you even a little excited?" she asked. "Sixteen is the best birthday ever."

I laughed at her enthusiasm, and as I reached back to fluff up my pillow I discovered a few remaining twinges from the last five days of camp. The camp's coaches sure hadn't cared about the record-setting heat and humidity. They had worked our butts off. Now I was ready for a little break before my own Northfield High coach, Mrs. Fortunata, could get her hands on me.

I looked to the other bed surprised that Tori was still asleep, then wondered if she was faking it so no one would bug her. If she really was sleeping, she had to be dreaming about some guy, since Tori was as boy crazy as anyone I knew. I grinned slyly at my sister. "Sneak over to Tori and whisper in her ear like you're Cooker, and tell her you love her and can't live without her." Lizzie started to giggle, but before she could hop off the bed, we heard an exasperated sigh and a pillow was thrown in our direction, something that Tori managed to do while still keeping her head firmly planted on the bed.

"I heard that, you beast. No happy birthdays for you," she said. She winked at my sister and then looked around the pink and white room, so girly-girl compared to mine. "Great room you got here, Lizzie. Where'd you sleep last night, anyhow?"

My sister sat up, pleased to be the center of Tori's attention. "Since Cooker was sleeping in Jackie's big bed, Mom let me sleep downstairs on the sofa all by myself. I got to watch TV 'til really late." Then she frowned, "You won't tell will you?"

"No way," Tori said, "but seriously, thanks for letting us use your room. You know," she said, looking around the room once more, "you can invite me to any of your sleepovers."

"Really?" my sister said excitedly. Lizzie adored Tori and why not. They were both princesses-in-training. Then Lizzie pouted and said in a sad, poor-me voice, "But I'm not allowed sleepovers yet. Daddy says not 'til fifth grade."

I cuddled my sister into me, saying, "Next year will be here before you know it." Then I looked over to Tori knowing she was not really a morning person and asked her how she was feeling.

She gave me the evil eye and grabbed her watch from the nightstand. "It's not even eight o'clock," She groaned, shifting her long, lanky frame around in the bed, probably trying to see if all her body parts were still working. Then she suddenly stopped. "Hey, how about us going undefeated?" she said excitedly.

"Pretty cool," I said, thinking about the nighttime competition the camp had for all the high school teams.

Tori was more alert now 'cause even royalty liked to win. "I think we're going to be pretty good this season," she said. "Was Becky awesome in goal or what?"

"Yeah, she was," I said. Then I glanced back down at my sister who was watching Tori's every move. "Tell Mom we'll be down in ten minutes. Okay?" She nodded reluctantly, not wishing to be out of her idol's presence for even a minute. Then she slid off the bed, giving Tori a little wave as she left the room.

I rolled over on my side to face Tori. "Glad Jules is going to be okay."

"Yeah, she was real relieved the doctor said it wasn't broken when I texted her last night. But two weeks rest and having to get around on crutches is going to make her a bear to live with."

"We've just gotta keep her entertained," I said, and began to stretch out the kinks in my muscles.

"Can't be me. I've got two modeling jobs in the city next week. Mom is taking me up on the train."

I stopped in mid-stretch at Tori's reference to her part-time work in New York. It was mostly catalog stuff, but at least it was a job. Something I was going to have to get real soon 'cause turning sixteen equaled a driver's permit which meant I was going to need spending money for gas.

Tori sat up and pulled her long dark hair up into a messy ponytail. She started rummaging through her cosmetic bag for the mirror that never seemed to be more than a few inches away since she'd become a model.

Jeez! Not another endless facial examination, Tori, I thought, as she kept staring into the mirror. She knew she was pretty with her big brown eyes, long lashes, and perfect skin that never fried. But when Tori started tugging at her face, moving her cheeks up and down with her hand, trying to look like one of those models in a magazine, I'd had enough.

"Hey, what about Chris," referring to the twins' gorgeous older brother. Can't he do stuff with Jules to keep her occupied?"

"Nah, he's working at Dad's basketball camp. Jules is on her own."

I resumed my stretching. "Well — I can keep her company." Getting no reaction, I suddenly reached over and snatched the mirror out of her hand. After a brief tussle back and forth, both of us laughing, I finally conceded the mirror back to Tori so she wouldn't suffer from 'reflection withdrawal.'

After one final look, she tossed the mirror back into her bag. "Camp **was** pretty amazing wasn't it?" she said, lying back onto the bed.

"It sure wasn't like last year," I said, remembering the snooty attitude of some of last year's seniors.

"Yeah, if it hadn't been for Mandy Stevenson being such a good captain we probably would have been eaten alive."

I turned onto my back, and stared up at the ceiling. Tori was right. Except for Mandy, who I had really liked, I was glad those seniors had graduated. They only thought the season should be about them, and most of last season had been pretty much of a mess because of it. Finally our coach had gotten fed up with their attitude and took a chance playing some of us younger players. We had tried our best, but we couldn't make it past the second round of the state tournament. I clenched my fists remembering the frustration we had felt at the end. *We had to do better this year — had to.*

"Hey," Tori said, "did you fall asleep or something?"

"No, just thinking."

"Well **I'm** thinking it's time for breakfast," Tori said, laughing as she rolled all five foot ten inches out of bed. She retied her knot of hair and turned to me expectantly.

"Okay, my stomach is grumbling too," I said, and hopped out of bed. "Race you." We pushed and shoved each other down the steps and out into the kitchen practically landing in a heap at my mom's feet.

"There you are. I was wondering when the two of you would make an appearance," Mom said, busy beating up something in a bowl. I peered around her arm. *Sweet! Pancakes!* She stopped for a moment, turned to give me a hug and wish me a happy birthday.

Avoiding her hands as she reached up to create some order to my crazy red curls, I asked where Cooker was. He had been my brother's overnight guest and had slept in my bedroom the night before which was why Tori and I had used Lizzie's room.

"They've already taken off for the shore," Mom said, turning back to her cooking. "They're staying overnight at Grandma McKendry's house. Matt promised Cooker some bodysurfing lessons before he heads home to New York."

I noticed Lizzie hopping back and forth from one foot to another. "She's dying to have you start your birthday celebration," Mom said, pointing her spatula to our kitchen table where a big envelope was propped against a giant bouquet of Gerber Daisies.

"Go ahead, open the envelope, before your sister explodes," Mom said.

I couldn't imagine what was inside. I had no special birthday requests. I touched the flowers' petals, their bright orange, purple, and red making me smile. There was an attached card which read 'Happy Birthday, Love Arianna, Don, and Chris Hanson.

"I looked up at Tori. "It was so nice of your family to remember my birthday. The flowers are my favorite"

"Glad you like them," Tori said. "Jules and I have something for you, too, but you'll get it later," she said, smiling at my confusion about her 'later' comment.

I picked up the envelope and Mom turned from the stove to watch me. It was a birthday card from my parents. Inside were some tickets. Puzzled at first, I looked more closely, then let out a scream that must have been heard up and down our block.

"I can't believe it!" I shrieked, dancing around the room. I looked at Tori who, from her expression, was already clued in to what was going on.

"Six tickets for tonight's Casey Collins and the Brewers concert," I screamed to everyone. They all laughed as I ran over to hug my mom. "Thanks so much. This is the best," I said. I studied the tickets again and asked who was going. Tori told me Jules, of course, and three other friends from the hockey team, Lindsay Sayers, Anna Merlino, and Ellen Burns. "They all knew?"

"Yep, pretty good secret," Tori said.

My mom turned to me. "Before you girls make too many plans, Jackie, I want to remind you that you need to watch Lizzie for about an hour on Monday. I have to get my fingerprinting done."

"Mrs. McKendry!" Tori said, puzzled. "Are you in trouble with the law or something?"

My mom laughed. "Not that I know of. But I am going to start substitute teaching this fall and fingerprinting is just part of all the paperwork you need to complete to be hired by the schools.

"You coming to our school?" Tori asked. "That'd be cool. I could show you around."

"I appreciate the offer, Tori," she said, "but I think I'll stick with the younger ones."

When Mom first approached the family with the idea of being a teacher again, she couldn't miss the look of horror that crossed my face at the possibility of having a parent in the same building as me. When she told me it was only for the elementary schools in our area I breathed a sigh of relief. Still it meant some real changes were going to happen in the McKendry household once school started. I only hoped they wouldn't affect me.

* * *

My birthday night was a blast. The twins bought me a Casey Collins T-shirt which immediately replaced the tank top I was wearing. Then the six of us, okay, well five since Jules wasn't much of a screamer, went nuts for almost two hours. Tori even walked up front like she owned the place conning some guard into getting me an autograph from the band. Through the laser lights and stage smoke I imagined it in a frame, sitting on my bureau.

After the concert, with Cooker gone, I had my own room back and as I was getting ready for bed, I was thinking sixteenth birthdays should be repeated over and over again 'cause this one had been just about perfect.

Super tired, I collapsed onto the bed, but I was so wound up from the concert that I couldn't sleep. I started doing a mental inventory of my summer vacation. It seemed like I did nothing but play hockey. In addition to the camp I had just come back from, my coach, Mrs. Fortunata, had pushed for Jules and me to learn as much as we could, so before the Virginia camp, Jules and I had attended two other camps on our own.

Someone at one of those camps must have liked our play 'cause then we were invited to a special tournament for hockey players that were going into their junior year. It was a pretty intense experience with a bunch of college coaches sitting around in their little beach chairs, watching us play. As the games went on, the coaches wrote notes on their clipboards that made some girls frantic thinking everything they did on the field was going to spell doom to their college careers, while others were wrapped up in their own stardom and never wanted to pass the ball. But college hockey seemed too far away to worry about, so I just played for fun, and figured anything that prepared me for the season at Northfield High had to be a good thing.

I finally gave up on sleep and decided to check my email. Camp had kind of kept me out of the electronic loop, and I was surprised by the amount of mail waiting for me. Opening each one, they all pretty much said the same thing — some college coach saw me play and thought I would be a good fit for their program, and please contact them, blah, blah, blah.

I laughed, shaking my head at the prank the twins had to be playing on me, sending this stuff. They must have thought it would get me all worked up and nervous to have to think about college already, and then later they could tell me to relax, that they had made it up. I fixed them, though, and pressed the delete key for all of the messages.

The next day the joke was on me. When I called Tori out on it, she said, "No, it's for real. Jules has been contacted, too." I couldn't tell my parents about this mistake. My dad would have gotten all upset, and my mom wouldn't have understood any of it, since she thought college was about getting an education, and maybe "finding a nice young man." I wondered if my goof-up would just blow over like some 'no harm-no foul' kind of thing or if it would turn into some major 'whoops.'

(3)

A few days later I rode my bike over to the twins' house. Most of my friends were 'Joe Average' when it came to money. One or two girls came from families that really had struggles like my teammate, Sam Jones, who couldn't afford to go to a single camp. The twins were different. Their mom was head of her own company and their dad was a workaholic basketball coach who owned a ton of camps. As I rounded the bend in the road, the 'Hanson Mansion' came into view. At least part of it did since there was a long drive with big old trees that hid most of the large Victorian house from the street.

The first time I had been in their house I had felt so uncomfortable and lost in its bazillion rooms that I almost hadn't come back to play with the twins. As I got to know them though, I realized they were like everybody else. They just had more stuff.

I dropped my bike by the Hanson's garage and walked around back. There was Jules in a red two-piece, sitting on the side of the family pool, her feet dangling in the water. As soon as she saw me she slipped beneath the water not emerging until she reached the far end of the pool.

She paused briefly to give me a wave and then pushed off the wall to break into a fast-paced freestyle. I took a seat on the steps at the shallow end of the pool and watched my friend churn through the water lap after lap. The doctor in the emergency room had told her "water exercise only," so I knew she was frustrated not being able to run and get herself ready for the season like the rest of the team.

After a few minutes her pace began to slow and she made her way over to me stretching out on the bottom step. She leaned back and shaded her eyes to look up at me. "Sorry," she said, "I just seem to have all this energy and no place to put it."

"Well, come on then. Maybe my job today is to tire you out."

For the next hour we played Marco Polo, dove for rings, and tried to see who could sit on the bottom of the pool longest without exploding to the top for air. We pretty much exhausted ourselves and finally we took to the chaise lounges to catch some late afternoon sun. I was looking forward to some real conversation about the hockey season when Jules' cell rang. It was Kate Carson and it seemed to me the call went on and on.

I woke a little while later to the splash of someone diving into the water and looked around in time to see Chris Hanson's head surfacing above the water at the other end of the pool. I had been his prom date last spring. No romance — just kind of helping him out of a jam when too many girls had asked him to the prom and he couldn't figure a way out of their invitations. I smiled remembering the evening's ending almost-kiss. I was pretty relieved it hadn't happened.

Back in sixth grade the twins and I had taken a 'pinkie blood swear,' a pinprick really, promising there would be no making goo-goo eyes at our older brothers. EVER! It was one of the few smart things we did that year. It just would have been way too messy to follow Chris around with puppy-dog eyes like so many girls did, so it was a vow I intended to keep.

Turning over on my side, I called, "Hey Chris, what's up? I thought you were working."

He didn't answer me at first. Instead he slid through the water to the side of the pool near where we were lying. As he hoisted himself out I was once again amazed as to how good looking he was, with his mom's dark Italian looks and his dad's brilliant blue eyes. Grinning, he stood over me and shook out his dark hair, dripping cold water all over me.

I shrieked as the cold water hit my skin. "No fair." Then I pretended to be mad and said, "You're a brute, Chris Hanson."

"Move over, Jackie. I promise to be good," he said softly.

I scooted over to make room for him and Jules finally ended the phone call. I guessed my shrieking had wakened her up to the fact I was still there.

"Camp over?" she asked her brother.

"Yep, all done," he said. "Dad's still there at school, finishing up some paperwork. Now I have to start thinking about what I need to take with me to college. Time's running out what with the trip and all."

"Jules said you're leaving for Italy," I said.

"Uh-huh. Day after tomorrow. I'm visiting our nana for two weeks. We've been planning a trip to the southern coast, near Pompeii, and then I come back and leave for school."

"Wow, so this is it. Are you excited about starting college?" I asked.

"I guess. I'll miss people here at home, especially you, of course," he laughed, teasing like he always did, "but I'm ready. The guys from the basketball team have already contacted me about getting together as soon as I hit campus."

"Tori and I are already making plans to go up this winter to see him play," Jules said.

"You'll have to bring 'the peanut' with you," he said, referring to my size of course. Then he said, "If there's not enough room in the car you can just shove her in a suitcase."

"Very funny!" I said, making a face at him.

His eyes crinkled up matching the warmth of his smile. "Gotta go. I'm meeting up with some of the guys." He stood up. "If I don't see you, Jackie, try not to break too many hearts this year."

"Oh, okay. Chris, I might say the same to you," I said, laughing at the idea of me breaking hearts. "But seriously, have a great time."

He gave me a long look, and as he walked toward the back door of the house he was whistling the same goofy, tuneless song that always made me think happy thoughts when I heard it.

Jules finally turned to me. "Tori told me about the emails. I can't believe you deleted them all. You should really contact those coaches."

"I don't even remember who they were."

Jules shook her head at my stupidity. "Maybe you should talk to Coach. She knows how it all works."

"How what works?"

"Are you kidding? All the stuff about college, the athletic scholarships, the recruiting, of course. I've already scheduled two college visits this fall."

I sat up suddenly and faced Jules. *How could she be talking about college? We hadn't even started our junior year.* "You're not serious, are you?" I said, feeling confused at Jules' interest in something other than the next few months. "How can you even think about some stupid college stuff when you ought to just bet concerned with the coming season?"

Jules started to make small circles in the air with her injured ankle trying to stretch the injured tissue. I thought from her expression that it must really hurt. Finally she stopped and let out a long breath."I can't believe you **even** said that. You of all people should know how much I care about this team."

"I didn't mean it like that. Jeez, Jules! But thinking about college is ridiculous right now."

"You're the one that's being ridiculous," she said hotly. "Maybe you need to wake up and think of your future."

I could feel my own temper starting to flare, so I snatched up my towel. I couldn't believe Jules was calling me out over stupid college stuff."I better go. Feel better," I said, and turned on my heels leaving her sitting in the chaise lounge. It was a long ride home.

(4)

The buzzing of my alarm clock signaled the end of summer vacation, at least for me. Even though there were still two weeks 'til school started, Coach was holding our first practice of the season that morning. As I finished dressing, I slipped into my favorite navy shorts, the same ones I had worn on the first day last year, and quietly made my way downstairs to grab a banana and a bottled water from the kitchen. As I sat on the front steps waiting for the twins' mom to pick me up, I felt excitement at the start of another season. But as the minutes passed, I began feeling a little anxious, too. My spat with Jules over the college thing had been bugging me for days. We really hadn't talked since that day at her pool and I just didn't know how to smooth things over.

Making our way across the school's parking lot to the fields, the silence between Jules and me continued. The only sound coming from her was the slow steady beat of her crutches hitting the asphalt. Suddenly, all I wanted was to sprint to the field and get lost in the routine of practice where I could pretend that everything was normal between us.

"Hey, guess what," Tori said, breaking into a little dance move. "We're halfway done high school, only one more 'first day of hockey' to go," she continued, as she pumped her fist in the air.

I turned to look at her. *First Jules with her college visits, now Tori. What was the sudden rush to get through high school?* Not that Tori wasn't right, of course, but saying it out loud made it kind of official, like it was all downhill from now on, just not the way I pictured our last two years of high school.

As we stepped onto the field I inhaled the smell of freshly mowed grass. It was like coming home. I looked around at the newly painted white lines marking the field, and then zeroed in on the semicircular line that defined the striking circle, the area at each goal where we could score goals. I began picturing the different ways I could cross that line and begin taking shots on goal, something I loved to do.

The field was a busy place that morning with dozens of girls trying out for the team. A few were already hitting balls to one another, and some were taking a jog around the field, while others were standing around the bleachers probably catching up on the latest summer gossip. I had known some of these girls all my life. It made my heart squeeze tight, 'cause after listening to the twins, I realized there was a clock ticking somewhere. I swore I could almost hear it saying — now or never, now or never.

Putting my gear down by the bench I noticed Ms. Gillespie, our assistant coach, sitting at the end of the bleachers jotting down notes on the clipboard that never seemed to leave her side. She was a math teacher at our school and looked more like a librarian, all prim and proper-like with her wireless glasses and quiet ways, than the former all-star goalkeeper that she actually was. She was a terrific coach who knew a ton about defense. The goalies loved her.

The final person to arrive at the field was Mrs. Fortunata, or 'Coach' as we all called her. As soon as we saw her coming across the field with our student managers, Brit and Nadja, the activity on the field cranked up a notch.

No one wanted to be caught not working hard even on the first day.

As she approached, Coach looked like she totally belonged on a sports field. No bigger than me, which isn't saying much, she had a compact frame with short salt-and-pepper hair that was never out of place. Every step she took seemed to have purpose and I could picture her, in her younger days, dashing down the field scoring winning goals.

There were a few words of welcome, and after Coach took us through our warm-ups we faced the hardest part of the morning — our annual timed three mile run. It was such a stressor for most of the players and everyone was always much happier when it was over. I looked at the younger players and could smell their nervousness as we lined up to begin the run at the far end of the field. I shook out my legs to keep them loose and then the whistle blew.

Coach made Becky Weiss, our goalkeeper, and me the pacers, our job being to lead the others past Dobber's farm, through a neighboring development, and then back to the school. We were first to cross the finish line and had already started our cool-down walk around the field when Becky said, "Be back in a few," and took off.

Five minutes later all of the runners seemed to be in and then I saw Becky walking across the school's parking lot to the finish line with a girl I didn't recognize. Becky spoke a few words to Ms. Gillespie, and then she jogged over to the bench to put on her goalie equipment. I walked over to her. "Where'd you go?"

"I decided to check on the younger players," she said. "You know how so many girls get freaked out about the run. Anyway, I found this girl on Evanine Drive tossing her cookies."

I looked over at the girl who was now talking to our trainer. She did look awfully pale. Then Coach blew the whistle for us fielders to join her at the far end of the field, and the girl was immediately forgotten.

At the end of practice I decided to be the first to break the ice, and went over to talk to Jules who had been sitting on the bench with her crutches for most of the practice. "Hey, Jules, what did you think of practice?"

She gave me a long stare like I had asked the wrong question, but then she said, "We seem to be further ahead of last year and a couple of the sophomores don't look bad at all."

Her answer seemed pretty positive, but I noticed she didn't look at me when she was talking. There was still that wall. I sat down next to her, slipped off my cleats, and grabbed my flip-flops from under the bench. I searched my mind for something that could make our conversation last. "How about the girl who came in so late in the run, do you know her?"

"Not really. Probably wasn't in shape. She'll be cut."

Jules sounded a little harsh. Wasn't she supposed to care about everyone? I gave Jules a second look, but she had already picked up her crutches and was hobbling over to Kate Carson.

For a moment I felt left out, like one of my best friends had found a new best friend and now our friendship had become yesterday's news. It was ridiculous to feel that way. I knew Jules had responsibilities to the team as a co-captain that didn't include me, but still ...

That night I couldn't sleep, thinking about Jules and Kate being co-captains. I knew being a captain was more than calling heads or tails at a pre-game coin toss, but did that mean old friendships should be forgotten? I didn't think so.

*   *   *

As we were warming up for practice the next day, I tried to pay some attention to some of the younger girls trying out for the team. Since Coach hadn't brought any of the freshmen up to varsity or JV last year, we really didn't know much about them.

There had been a few sophomores that had gone to camp with us, but they had kept pretty much to themselves. We had tried to be nice and had even invited them to walk into town with us for ice cream one night, but they passed on it.

On camp's traditional skit night, each class having to do a take-off on a famous TV show, I thought things would get better and the classes would get closer 'cause it sure had been a hilarious evening. My class had done our version of "American Idol." Tori, Jules, and Lindsay played the original judges. Jules pretended to be the notorious Simon Cowell, Tori — Paula Abdul, and Lindsay played Randy Jackson.

I had to be one of the contestants which made me nervous 'cause I hated performing in front of people. Even when we were practicing the skit with just the other juniors, I sang so softly no one could hear me. A few of the girls said it wasn't working and maybe I shouldn't do it. A part of me felt relieved that I was getting out of it. Then Anna spoke up and thought it would be cool if we did the act like we were twins that couldn't be separated and had to try out for the show together.

The only thing Anna and I had in common was our size — we were the two smallest girls on the team. One look at her sleek, dark hair, nothing like my crazy red curls, would be a dead give-away that we couldn't be related so I didn't know how it would work. I should have remembered Tori's many talents.

Besides being a part-time model, Tori was super artistic, so she got to work and waved her magic wand. The night of the skit Anna and I were in matching outfits crafted by Tori. Our hair was pulled up and hidden under large baseball hats that we had flipped around. Our look was completed with huge dark glasses and matching beauty marks, another Tori creation.

When Anna and I looked at the finished results in the mirror I had to smile. We did look like sisters. With Anna by my side I felt more confident and even clowned around a little when we performed. We weren't the hit of the show though, Becky was. Always the comedian, she played one of those terrible singers who went on the show just because they wanted their face on TV.

The sophomores did a takeoff on some vampire show I'd never heard of so I didn't get it although their makeup was cool. Everyone else laughed though. I thought that after all of the skits were done and everyone had loosened up we'd be one big team. But we weren't. The sophomores faded into the background as soon as the night was over.

Now that we were back at school, the younger players still didn't seem to be any more noticeable, and I doubted there would be any sophomore who would rise up and make a difference in our season. I looked around the field and could see why. Half the players trying out were juniors. Not only had we played together since freshmen year, but had survived a freshman hazing together that none of us would ever forget. That whole experience had seemed to bind us together in a way that not even the few seniors on the team could penetrate. Jules and Kate, as captains, seemed to be the exceptions.

As I waited my turn for the next drill, I glanced over at Jules who was busy chatting quietly with Kate and felt a pang in my chest. I knew it was stupid, but it had always been me and Jules when it came to hockey. Now it seemed I was being replaced. I mean there was still Tori, but Tori considered hockey a 'recreational activity,' something to do in the afternoons until all the cute boys were available to call her at night. Hockey was something I didn't think I could live without and I didn't know anyone on the team who felt like that except Jules. All of a sudden the upcoming season seemed to get a little more lonely.

After a few more drills, Coach told us to pick a partner for a full-field passing drill in which we'd pass the ball back and forth with our partner as we moved from one end of the field to the other. I automatically thought of Jules who had always been my partner in the past, but then remembered she was stuck with crutches, sitting on the sideline. For a moment I felt paralyzed with indecision. *Now what?* Then Coach yelled for everyone to hurry up. She saw me still standing there and said, "Jackie, Cassie needs a partner. Grab a ball and get in line."

I hurried over to the ball bag and saw a girl shyly standing off to the side. I was pretty sure she was the girl who'd gotten sick the day before. She looked scared to death. "Come on," I said. "We don't want to be the last ones down the field."

While we were waiting in line behind the other pairs, I studied the girl. She was staring at the players already going down the field like she was trying to memorize everything she was seeing, and she was gripping the stick all wrong. *What's the matter with her? Everyone knows how to hold the stick.*

When it was our turn, I started with the ball and said, "Go," expecting her to take off down the field and then I'd hit her the ball. She hesitated until I repeated the command and then she took off. Boy, she was fast! She caught up with the ball, but then she stopped it with the rounded side of her stick, a big no-no in field hockey.

I shook my head in frustration. This wasn't ice hockey. A field hockey stick had a right side and a wrong side for playing the ball. It's what made the game such a challenge and it's what every athlete learned as soon as they picked up a stick. As I took off down the field I hoped she'd at least give me a decent pass back. No such luck. Our whole turn was stop-and-go all the way down the field and we were the last twosome to get to the other end of the field. My face was red with embarrassment as the whole team was waiting for us so they could begin the drill once again back to where we had all started.

"Sorry," the girl stammered, as we waited at the end of the lines. I looked over to her and saw the tears in her eyes.

"That's okay," I said, pretending it wasn't the big deal it really was. As we moved up toward the front of the line, I thought more about what had just happened. She looked athletic enough and definitely had speed so what was up with the 'no skill at all bit'?

Finally I said, "You played freshman ball last year, right?"

She shook her head. "I just moved here from Tennessee. My high school didn't have hockey." She saw I was still listening, so she continued. "I like to run." She saw the shocked expression on my face. "Yeah, I know … yesterday, nervous stomach I guess. Anyhow when my parents registered me for classes we met Mrs. Fortunata in the office and we got to talking. She said I could try out. I think maybe I made a mistake. It's harder than it looks."

I felt like a jerk. Here she was a beginner trying to fit in with girls that already had five or six years of hockey under their belts. Now that I heard her speak I could tell she was from someplace else. It made me think of other people I had known that had to change schools and how hard it must have been to start all over again.

Suddenly it didn't matter that she couldn't tell one side of the stick from the other. I was going to help her. At least until she got cut. I didn't see how she could make it in our program since we were pretty strong and it was obvious she didn't have any skill.

"Look," I said, "How about if I help you — where do you live?" When she told me, I realized she lived just four blocks from my house, so I invited her over for that very afternoon.

The next day I kept an eye on Cassie throughout practice. She was better and I could see her confidence building. I just didn't know if it was good enough not to be cut. We had made arrangements for her to come over my house after practice one more time as cuts would be coming after the next day's practice.

While the twins and I were waiting in the parking lot for my mom to pick us up, I asked Jules, "How many girls do you think coach is cutting?"

She shrugged her shoulders. "Ten or fifteen, I guess," she said. "I don't know why some of them even came out. They obviously didn't work out much."

"Who's that girl you were partnering up with yesterday?" Tori asked, as she skipped through her cell phone looking for messages. "She was awful."

"Cassie's never played before," I said, feeling like I needed to defend her.

Jules' eyes grew large in surprise. "Why would she ever try out then?" she asked.

"Maybe to fit in at Northfield. She just moved here, and, besides, Coach said she could," I said. "Anyway you have to give her props for trying."

"Yeah, you're right," Jules said. "But I don't hold out much hope."

I had to agree with Jules on that one and decided I'd really have my work cut out for me in the afternoon when Cassie came over for her second lesson.

*   *   *

After the next morning's practice, players rushed to the gym to check out the magic 'you made it' list. For the first time as a player I didn't break out in a sweat. I knew I'd make the team so I hung back letting the others have their chance to look. I saw Cassie edging her way through the crowd forming around the bulletin board and read down the list. When she slowly backed away, I held my breath to see what I was sure would be the disappointment on her face.

To my surprise there was no reaction. Instead she seemed to be looking around for someone, and then she spotted me standing under a tree. The biggest grin broke out on her face, and if I live to be a hundred I will never forget that smile. I gave her a 'thumbs up' and felt my heart expand. Maybe Coach would have picked her anyway. She **did** have speed, but I know in some small way I helped, too.

"What are you so happy about?" Tori asked as I joined the twins sitting on the curb waiting for our ride.

"Cassie Henry made it," I said.

"I didn't think she had a chance," Jules said, as she pulled at a lone blade of grass that had insisted on growing through a crack in the pavement. "But I guess Coach knows what she's doing. Anyway the main thing is we now have our team."

When my mom pulled up with Lizzie in tow, I followed Tori into the back seat, sandwiching myself once again between the twins. I leaned back against the seat and closed my eyes. This is the way it should always be — the three of us, best buds forever. I sent up a little prayer to the hockey gods that everything would somehow get back to normal with Jules and me. I glanced at Jules, but she was staring out the window and seemed a million miles away.

(5)

With a week left of practice the main topic among the returning players was who would start for Northfield. As much as Coach tried to disguise her thinking, switching players around, she couldn't fool us. We knew the forward line would be the same as last year — Tori, Sam Jones, and me. Our defensive backs were, Jules, of course, once she got back on the field, Lindsay Sayers, another junior, and Jess Piotrowski, a senior who had patiently waited to finally have her time on varsity. With Anna in the deepest defensive position as sweeper, and Becky in goal, our defense was looking mighty strong.

The only question mark seemed to be one of the three midfield positions. Kate Carson and Heather Whitcraft, a bubbly blond junior, would return to their varsity positions from last year, but the third position was up for grabs. Coach was looking at a bunch of people and no one was standing out.

The possible lineups were rolling through my mind as I rode with the Hansons to practice. Tori was behind the wheel with her brand new probationary driver's license. Both twins had passed the test the day before, and couldn't wait to cruise out on their own.

Mrs. Hanson was sitting next to Tori and seemed totally relaxed with her daughter behind the wheel. I could just picture my own mom, hands braced against the dashboard and feet firmly pushing through the floorboards, not trusting me a bit. I looked over to Jules to see how she was judging her sister's driving, but she seemed distracted, picking at her nails, something she rarely did.

"What's the matter?" I asked.

"The trainer is going to test me today to see if I can start running."

"That's awesome."

"Yeah, but if he doesn't let me I'll be that much further behind. He has me on the bike, but that's not the same as running. Besides, I need to be out there," she said, clenching her fists.

For a moment I forgot I might not be her best friend anymore. "We could stay after practice for awhile and I could help you with your stick work," I said hopefully.

"Thanks, Jackie. We'll see," she said.

As soon as we got to the school Jules went off in search of the trainer. "Don't mind Jules," Tori said, as we walked toward the field. "She's been a crank-pot ever since she got hurt." She draped her arm around my shoulder. "Besides, you've still got me."

I smiled up at her. She was right. She was my friend, too. It was just that she really didn't share my passion for hockey and I knew once school started and Tori found her next boyfriend, I would be put on the back burner for awhile.

Halfway through practice I noticed Jules coming out of the gym. I tried to make eye contact with her, but she was looking for someone else. It was Kate. The two smiled at each other and I saw Jules give Kate the okay sign. I blinked and then a ball smacked me on the leg. All of a sudden I felt like second best and it just wasn't the ball hitting my shin that hurt.

* * *

The day of our first scrimmage, an away match, I was leaning against the side of the school bus a few feet from the door, letting some of the younger players get on board ahead of me. As they passed by me the excitement of the day radiated off their skin. It was contagious and I started feeling my own nerves start to catch the fire until Lindsay tapped me on the back.

"Why are you letting them cut in front?" she said.

I understood Lindsay's concern 'cause where a person sat on the bus for the away games was almost as important as who sat at your table for lunch. A tradition at Northfield was for upperclassmen to have the back and now that finally meant us.

"Don't worry," I said, "Jess Piotrowski and Tori got on the bus first. They'll make sure the sophomores know to sit near the front." Then I followed Anna up the steps, carefully stepping over the minefield of the younger players' gear as we made our way to our prime location. Noticing the seat next to Tori was already taken I settled in next to Anna and shoved my stick bag under the seat.

As the bus lurched forward I snapped my fingers suddenly remembering something and reached down to my stick bag double checking if I had my mouth guard for the game. I let out a sigh of relief when I found it tucked away in an inner pocket of my bag. As the bus pulled onto the main road I looked around the back of the bus and had a moment of panic as I realized for the first time that Jules wasn't there and neither was Kate. I almost yelled, "Stop! Wait!" And then I saw them, sitting at the front right next to the coaches.

Lindsay leaned across the aisle nodding toward the front of the bus and whispered, "Too good for us now."

Without thinking I snapped back, "Don't be silly." It was a typical 'Lindsay comment' when it came to Jules and it went both ways. Jules and Lindsay had been rubbing each other the wrong way since elementary school and I figured it was just two strong personalities bumping heads. I tried to put what Lindsay said out of my mind, but it kept twisting its way back into my thinking. Maybe Lindsay had something. Maybe Jules was so wrapped up on being a captain with Kate that the rest of us juniors weren't so important anymore. I closed my eyes and pretended to catch up on some sleep.

Once on the field we put our gear under the benches and went through our normal warm-up routine, psyched to show off what we could do. Things went our way right from the start and by the second half we had built a 4-0 lead. Then Coach began to sub some of us. Sitting on the bench, watching the others, I thought it had been almost too easy, but I had been so happy to be out on the field again against some real competition that I didn't see how it might affect our team down the line.

On the ride home Jules and Kate made their way to the back of the bus which meant all the rest of us had to shift around. "Hey guys," Kate said, smiling, "we did great today. Just keep it up in the next scrimmage and we'll be ready for the season." She looked a little nervous like she really didn't know what else to say. Finally she turned to Jules.

That's it. That's all you're going to say. I was disappointed. This was our senior captain. Where was the inspiration, the fire?

I noticed Lindsay roll her eyes when Jules began to speak. "If we're going to have a good season I think we should talk about what we think the team needs to do so we're all on the same page. We need to make a goal for the season now."

I perked up. What Jules said finally made sense. We did have to want the same thing. That was the trouble with last year's team. Too many people wanted the season to be about them and not the team.

Jules went on, "Becky, you're the goalie. What do you think?"

Becky started talking about us guarding the opposing players tighter near the goal and not letting them get to her pads so easily so she'd have more room to maneuver and get to the ball. Then the discussion started to flow. Maybe us older players talked for ten minutes and anybody that wanted a say had a chance to speak. I just listened 'cause Jules pretty much said what I was already thinking. After it was over one or two of my teammates pulled out a book, while most others continued to chat with the player next to them. A few like me slipped on their head phones. I wondered if they were thinking about today's scrimmage. I closed my eyes and replayed the team's conversation. It was good that people talked about what we needed to fix on the field, but we still hadn't said what we wanted as a team. Was everyone afraid to say it? And if we couldn't say it out loud to each other could it ever possibly come true?

(6)

It was the first day of school, and after I put in new studs, a birthday gift from Grandma McKendry, I stopped to admire the moss-green sparkle of the peridot stones in the bedroom mirror. That's when I noticed the piece of paper taped to a corner of the mirror in my mom's handwriting. *Must have snuck in after I went to bed,* I thought, as I examined the paper more closely. It turned out to be what my mom had labeled 'my junior year to-do list.' My eyes traveled down the sheet — SAT Class, then Behind The Wheel, an on-the-road class for probationary drivers. Next she had listed Part-time Job and Better Grades. What a Debbie Downer my mom could be! *Where did it say have fun, be with my friends, and play hockey, Mom?*

I flicked a finger on the paper. My own list for junior year wouldn't need any writing down. It was tattooed on my heart. Win a State Championship, of course, and …

I pulled open the drawer of my bureau, and then reached toward the back, feeling for the package wrapped in tissue paper. Inside was the bracelet that my one, and so far, only boyfriend, Mitch Kennedy, had given me when we were freshmen. Mitch and I had been together for a whole year, and then one day last fall he was pulled out of school when his military father, with whom he was living, suddenly was called overseas. That meant he had to return to Texas to live with his mom.

I had missed him terribly, especially our nightly talks on the phone discussing our day and the stuff that really mattered to us. A year later he was still not gone from my heart. Sometimes I would catch myself wondering how he was doing and who he might be doing it with. I didn't let myself dwell on those kinds of thoughts for long, though. They were just too painful. I shoved the bracelet back into its resting place and shut the drawer. It was going to be a new school year. I needed to put the past behind me.

Sitting on the rickety school bus with its cheesy brown seats I longed for the rides to school my brother used to give me and wondered if by next year I could be driving myself to school. But that would require a car and that would require a job. I slid down in my seat. It wasn't easy getting older. Not easy at all.

When the bus pulled into the parking lot I pulled a folded sheet of paper out of my backpack and quickly scanned my class schedule stopping at the only things that truly mattered — third period gym and sixth period lunch. There was only one problem with my schedule — it was 'twin-less.' Even though I wasn't brainy like Jules or some major art genius like Tori, I had always been lucky enough to connect with one of them sometime during the school day. And, as I stepped off the bus and followed the other students streaming into the building, one thing I knew for sure, it was going to be a long day 'til practice without one of my two best buddies by my side.

After second period I hurried to the gym. When I got there I busted out my first genuine smile of the day. Sitting in the first row of bleachers were Anna Merlino and Sam Jones. I joined them and together we watched the other students filing in. My heart skipped a beat when I noticed an old nemesis, Emma Connors, waltz through the far gym door. She was draped all over Kurt Evans, a basketball teammate of Mitch's. Emma had tried to hook Mitch for herself back in ninth grade. Since that hadn't worked, maybe she was going to make her way through the other guys on the team. My eyes narrowed at my thoughts and I let out a hiss.

Sam gave me a nudge. "What's wrong, Jackie?"

I didn't answer right away so absorbed as I was watching Emma making her grand entrance. She had paused by the door for just a moment and was now slinking across the gym floor like 'here I am, aren't I special.' I supposed a guy would call her sexy, with her long, long tanned legs and short skirt. Her straight blond hair swayed from side to side as she moved toward us and I unconsciously put a hand to the springy strands of hair that were trying to escape from my ponytail and realized I would never have hair that would move like that.

I glanced around the gym. I wasn't the only pair of eyes fastened on Emma. Half the boys in the gym were, too. As she climbed the steps of the bleachers heads turned. She turned around and scanned the gym, probably giving her subjects one final look before she sat her royal self down.

Sam touched my arm and I suddenly remembered her question. "Sorry. That girl and I," I said, thumbing toward Emma, "we've had a few run-ins that's all."

Sam's eyes widened, and then she laughed. "Hope you left marks."

I leaned back against the bleachers chuckling to myself. *Can't beat a teammate's loyalty, even off the field.*

One of the gym teachers blew his whistle to call us to order which was no easy task as there were over a hundred of us packed into the bleachers. As he took attendance he divided us into three smaller groups, and as we were shuffled around the bleachers into our new groups I saw my freshmen hockey coach, Ms. O'Donnell, entering the gym. Only in her third year at Northfield just like my buddies and me, we had gravitated to her right from the beginning.

When she stopped in front of our group, Sam, Anna, and I grinned. She was going to be our teacher. Gym was going to be the coolest class ever, except for one thing. Emma and Kurt had moved with us, too, and now they were seated just a few yards away. I heard them talking and was sure I heard my name and some snickering. I felt my ears grow warm and my temper start to flare.

Sam looked back at Emma, so she had heard it, too. Then Sam made a motion like she was picking something unpleasant off of her sweatshirt and made like she was grinding it under her sneaker. I refused to look at her 'cause I would have burst out laughing. I knew my thoughts weren't so very nice at that moment and hoped they wouldn't have a way of turning back on me.

Anna, Sam, and I found that we also had lunch together so we made a plan to meet up later, with Anna volunteering to find us a table since she had a class just a few doors down from the cafeteria. By the time sixth period arrived I was starving. I quickly stashed my books in my hall locker and hurried to lunch. It was already a mob scene by the time I arrived. Long lines everywhere, I decided the quickest food fix was going to be the school's overlooked salad bar.

Rabbit food in hand, I spotted Anna seated at a corner table talking to a guy whose back was to me. As I approached the table there was something about him that seemed vaguely familiar.

Anna glanced up and waved. "Hey, Jackie. You know Will, right?"

I nodded and managed to plaster a smile on my face when Will Standley looked up. He had been Mitch's closest friend and seeing him again brought back all the memories of when Mitch and I were together.

Will didn't return my smile. From the look he gave me it seemed like I was the last person he wanted to share a lunch table with. I felt stupid standing there when he didn't say anything, so I just plopped down my tray and took a seat.

"What's up?" I asked, snatching a piece of lettuce that was about to fall off my plate, wondering all the while how he and Anna knew each other and what the heck was up with his obvious coolness toward me.

He shrugged. "Not much. How about you?"

Before I could answer, a familiar voice behind me said, "Hey, can we join you guys?"

It was Noah Hart, who Tori and I had shared a lunch table with last year. A little blond had her arm around Noah's waist, and from the adoring look she was giving him, I figured she must be his latest girlfriend. Noah was part of an alternative band that included James Blount, Jules' boyfriend. Jules and James had met at a concert that the band had given about a year ago, and they had been together ever since.

As Noah took a seat, it dawned on me that he was now a senior which was hard to imagine when you saw him for the first time. He could have been easily mistaken for a freshman having his first day of high school with his slight build and baby face.

After our first hunger pangs were satisfied we launched into the necessary meet and greets and just a few minutes later there were more introductions when Sam joined us. Nothing much had changed about Sam since the first day I had met her two years ago, at least not on the outside. In fact she was wearing the same faded navy sweats, still with no makeup, and hair pulled severely back, as it was everyday, in a simple ponytail. We had started out badly as freshmen teammates. But we had mended our differences by the end of our first season together and now there was no one I'd rather have playing next to me than her.

As I was gnawing on an apple it came to me that I was sitting amidst a group of people that were complete strangers to me not so long ago. Not one of them was connected to my old life at Washington Elementary. For a moment it felt like a door was closing behind me and my only option was to move forward, like it or not. I only hoped it didn't exclude the twins.

The last class of the day was Honors English. It was my best class. Actually it was the only class I liked, besides gym. Upon entering the room, I scanned the first few rows for a familiar face, and then spotted James Blount sitting in the last row. He saw me, too, and motioned me back to an empty seat next to him. He was still sporting a little onyx stud in one ear, but his unruly hair had grown longer, almost covering the tattoo he had on the back of his neck. He was definitely not the type you would picture Jules with unless you got to know him. He was super bright like Jules and she seemed to appreciate his talent as a singer. In some strange way it worked for them, although to me it seemed like their relationship was more about being good friends than a 'love me 'til the end of time' kind of thing.

James and I did a quick summer run through — he working with his band on weekends and taking a music theory course at a local college, me being a jock at all my hockey camps and visiting Grandma McKendry at the shore on my free weekends.

While our English teacher, Mrs. North, was handing out our semester reading lists and a bunch of other papers that spelled more work, I noticed James scanning a sheet that said

'Vocabulary Words for the SATs'. He glanced up and asked me, "So you thinking about what you want to do for college?"

I crossed my eyes and made a sour face. He laughed, but held my gaze, expecting an answer. I tried to be flip. "As little as possible," I said.

But James was not a person to let things go easily when he really wanted to know something. When he didn't laugh at my attempt to blow off his question, I sighed and gave in. "I don't want to think about college. I just really want to enjoy right now," I said. I hated the whine in my voice, but I was trying to be honest with James as he had always been with me. I began turning up the edges of the vocabulary sheet debating about something more and then I said, "Don't laugh. I think I'd kind of like to be a coach."

I felt so vulnerable. I had never told anyone about this. I looked at James. He nodded thoughtfully. "I bet you'd be terrific, Jackie," he finally said.

I glanced down at my handouts. The print seemed a little blurry. James hadn't laughed. He thought I could actually do it.

(7)

As the days ticked away toward our final scrimmage, Mrs. Fortunata was really pushing the conditioning, piling on the sprints, and people were starting to complain. Even I was feeling it, and couldn't wait to crawl into bed every night. On top of that my teachers must have had a team meeting and decided to have a contest to see who could outdo the other with homework assignments. I felt like I'd been in school for months instead of just a couple of days.

The day of the scrimmage I woke to the sound of raindrops splattering against the window. I swung my feet out of bed and let out a groan. The weather made every ache from the last few days' work feel so much worse.

As I made my way over to the window I could feel the stiffness in my quads from all of our suicide drills and knew I was going to have to stretch really well to be ready for the afternoon. I peered out the window to our back garden and wondered how rain could be so good for the flowers and be so unwanted by a high school athlete. I stood there, my nose against the window, willing the rain to go away, maybe to some place like the Australian Outback or the Sahara Desert.

By sixth period lunch the rain had not let up, and the weather became the main topic of conversation. "What'll happen if we can't play?" We open in a few days," I said, as

I stared out the cafeteria windows for some sign of the sun peaking through the clouds.

Will Standley looked up from of his latest paperback and said, "You need to chill. It's just a scrimmage, right?"

"If it was a basketball scrimmage I bet it would matter then," Sam said to Will, sending him a dark look.

"Maybe," Will said reluctantly. "But in basketball we never get rained out. You guys should have stuck with an indoor sport."

That struck a nerve and I thought he was being a jerk. Even Anna, normally so easy going, narrowed her eyes at him. He must have noticed 'cause he said, "Jeez, can't you guys take a joke."

He might have been joking, but I know if Mitch had been there nothing would have been said. It reminded me how much my old boyfriend had understood how much hockey meant to me. I guess I had been spoiled.

I noticed Anna watching Will who was hiding once again behind his book. I wondered if she was interested in Will and if his remark had given her second thoughts. He glanced at her over the rim of the book and squirmed a little in his seat. It got me thinking, if the attraction went both ways, there might be a little heart hovering above our table with a big question mark on it.

When the bell rang I made a beeline for the cafeteria exit. I was anxious to get to study hall so I could finish my homework for eighth period English. In the crowded hallway I accidently bumped into someone causing me to drop one of my books. After I scurried around a few people trying to make up the time lost retrieving my book, I noticed a dark haired boy, taller than all the rest, turn a corner and disappear down another hallway.

I began to hyperventilate, and leaned against the wall letting people pass in front of me. I suddenly felt cold and clammy. It had to be a mistake, but I could have sworn the boy was Mitch Kennedy.

I slumped into a seat in the back of the auditorium waiting for the study hall teacher to take roll. Closing my eyes, I tried to process what I had just seen. I went over it again and again. It had to be a coincidence just 'cause I had been thinking about him at lunch. That's what I convinced myself, and besides, I thought, *if Mitch had really returned from Texas, he'd be calling me for sure. Wouldn't he?*

In English I tried to get the nagging feeling out of my head that somehow Mitch had come back to Northfield. I passed a note to James.

Hey – Did you ever see someone that looked so much like someone you knew it gave you goosebumps?

He glanced over at me and must have seen the question wasn't a casual one. His pen hovered over the paper for a moment, and then he turned the paper over and wrote —

Yeah, it's a creepy feeling — but sometimes if you get another look you know you got it all wrong and it's nothing like the person you thought it was.

I smiled back at him. He was right. I had only gotten a glimpse — really just the back of the guy's head. I was just being stupid. I needed to keep it real. Mitch was gone for good.

Just before the bell rang an announcement came over the intercom. Our scrimmage was canceled. *Bummers!* Only the varsity was to report to the gym for a short practice. I knew what that meant — wind sprints.

When I got to the locker room I found Jules and Kate deep in conversation. A few minutes later they called the rest of us over to the bench where they were sitting.

"What's up," Becky asked as she struggled with the buckles on her goalie kickers.

"They've canceled the scrimmage," Kate said.

"Yeah, we already know," Lindsay said, as she tried to balance the end of her stick on her finger tips without it crashing to the ground.

Jules gave her an impatient look. "And they're **not** rescheduling it."

That surprised us all. It meant this was it. We had no more competition until our season opened and we needed to practice our set plays. Who was going to take penalty strokes? Coach still hadn't even handed out our uniforms. The list of 'we're **so** not ready yet' was getting longer and feelings of panic were starting to set in.

"Hey," Tori said, glancing up at the locker room clock, "we better get out to the gym or we'll be late."

When we got there Mrs. Fortunata and Ms. Gillespie were waiting along with piles of navy kilts, navy shirts, white shirts, sweats and cold-weather gear. Coach sat us in the bleachers and explained that they couldn't find another date to have the scrimmage and what was important now was to make every moment count. Then she handed out paper bags with our names already on them and we lined up, seniors first, going down the rows of piles arranged by sizes, and picked out what we needed. I was shocked how fast it went. We had to have the most organized coaches in the world.

We stacked our bags on the bleachers. As I put mine down I glanced inside at my uniform shirt with my old number two and touched it for luck. For a split second I pictured myself wearing it with a state tournament trophy in my hands.

Surprisingly coach didn't have us do wind sprints that day. Instead she introduced a drill called 'continuous.' She put us in teams of three and we played from one end of the gym to the other in a 3v2, hopping out when we scored or lost the ball and coming back on the floor a minute or two later. It was fast paced, exhausting, and fun. Coach was **so** smart. It was just what we needed to get over our disappointment of not having the scrimmage.

At the end of practice she brought us in to the center of the gym and outlined everything we were going to work on in the next few practices. She had it all covered — the set pieces, the strokes. Everything we had worried about was taken care of.

As we waited for the four-thirty buses to arrive I turned to Jules, who for once was not engrossed in conversation with Kate Carson, probably because Kate had gotten a ride home with another senior. I said to her, "Awesome practice today considering we couldn't play."

She smiled back at me like the old Jules, like all the times in the past when we were on each other's wavelength. "Yeah, it was a good one. Say, I guess you know this, but I saw ..."

She was interrupted when Tori ran up to us. "Quick," she said to her sister, "we got a ride home with the guy from my chemistry class." She winked at me, "This could be lucky number seven," referring to the number of boyfriends she had had since eighth grade. Jules gave me an apologetic wave as Tori pulled her toward the waiting car.

As I boarded my bus I wondered why things were always changing in my life, why people and their friendships didn't always stay the same. I had thought about telling Jules and Tori about my silly imaginings about seeing Mitch in the hallway, but had changed my mind. They probably weren't interested in hearing about it anyway.

(8)

On my way to study hall on Monday my hallucination happened again — a tall, dark-haired boy turning a corner and disappearing down the hall. I tried to catch up to get a better look, but he must have moved into one of the science rooms, for when I got to the corner he was nowhere in sight. I thought I must be really losing it now 'cause this was two days in a row. I decided I was probably wishing so hard for my old boyfriend to return to Northfield that I was now conjuring up images of him and placing them onto any tall, dark-haired boy in the school. I laughed at myself and figured I better google 'over-active imagination' when I got home that night.

However, at practice I found out I wouldn't need to consult any computer. Lindsay came up to me on a water break. "Hey, I just saw Mitch Kennedy in my lunch today, looking yummier than ever I might add. You guys back together or what?"

Lindsay kept talking. I know it 'cause I saw her mouth moving, but I had no idea what she was saying. I felt myself falling down a big hole, one that had no end. I hadn't been losing my mind. I had seen him. Questions flew at me — *Why hadn't he called? Did he forget my number? Was it really that I didn't matter anymore?* The thought broke my heart into a million pieces.

I don't know how I got through the rest of practice. I felt like a robot just going through the motions. For once I couldn't wait to get out of there.

When I got home from practice there was some mail waiting for me on the hall table. It was a postcard, and for a moment my broken heart sounded a happy beat as it recognized the backwards scrawl of Chris Hanson. I was super surprised he took time out of his new college life to wish me well in our first game later that week. "Score one for me," he had written.

After dinner I called Tori and told her I had heard from her brother.

"Yeah, I just got off the phone with him. He said he sent you something."

"How's he doing?" I asked, trying to keep things light as I started stripping off my socks and tossing them in the ever growing pile of dirty clothes sitting in a corner of my room.

"He's loving it," she said. "He's met all the guys on the basketball team and they're already working out together.

"Has he got a girlfriend yet," I asked, thinking how his good looks must be attracting every girl on campus.

"Who knows? He's pretty closed-mouth when it comes to the romance department. But … speaking of romance, that guy who took us home is …" Tori was off and running with her newest possible, yet still too early to tell, love interest.

Even though we were talking on the phone I could picture the sparkle in her eyes and the acceleration of her pulse. Tori was in love with love. But she wasn't a 'collector' like some people I knew, like a certain Emma Connors.

Then I got to the real reason I called. "Mitch is back," I said.

"Yeah, I know. Jules said he came back on Friday. He's in two of her AP classes. We figured you knew and just didn't care anymore. I mean it's been a long time and all."

At first I was angry that Tori hadn't told me right away, and then I realized Tori was just being Tori. She was always able to mend Monday's broken heart by Friday. But that didn't excuse other people who knew he was back. I was going to get to the bottom of things.

*   *   *

The next day I rushed out of my fifth period class, almost on a dead sprint to the cafeteria. Even the threat of a detention for running in the halls couldn't have stopped me. I needed answers and I knew exactly who had them. Fortunately he and Anna were the only ones at the table. "Why didn't you tell me?" I said, slamming my books down on the table. Will turned eyes wide and mouth open in surprise, and then his face grew cold and his mouth tightened.

"What's this about?" Anna looked at the two of us in confusion.

Will shrugged. "What does it matter?"

The others were joining us now and Will tried to end the conversation by opening a paperback. But I didn't care. I needed to know. I sat down next to him and pulled at his arm. "Will ..." I said again.

"Okay, okay. He's back. There ... happy?"

"No. I'm not happy that I didn't know, that nobody told me." *That he didn't call,* I thought.

Will started to turn away. No one said a word. Then Will swung back in his seat and faced me again. "What do you care, anyway? You moved on soon enough when you hooked up with Hanson."

"That's not true," I blurted out, stunned that he could think I blew off his best friend as soon as he left Northfield.

"Did you or did you not go to St. Benedict's prom with Chris Hanson?" he challenged.

"Yes, but …," I couldn't finish. What could I say? Tell him the only reason I did it was to get Chris out of a jam, that his sisters' practically begged me to do it? That was something private and would have been embarrassing for anyone else to know the truth, so I said nothing. After a few moments it was so uncomfortable sitting there that I finally got up and said, "I'm going. The bell's going to ring soon." I stood by the cafeteria door waiting for the period to end and looked back at the table which was in a very animated conversation. I needed to get out of there. I needed time to think.

*   *   *

I was oblivious to my teammates' happy chatter as we made our way out of the locker room to the hockey field that afternoon. I was lost in my thoughts of Mitch. *All this time I had been wishing for Mitch to be back at Northfield, but not like this.* I had been picturing some kind of walking hand-in-hand happy reunion, not no word to me like I didn't matter. What could I look forward to now?

That night I was aimlessly thumbing through my desk and came upon the calendar I had hanging in my room a year ago. It was one of those school calendars that started in July and ended the following June. I had almost thrown it out at the end of sophomore year. I smiled at the big red star I had drawn for the first day of hockey camp, and then as I flipped through the pages came to some more difficult reminders of sophomore year. *Why had I kept it?* I tried to think back to the day in June when I was throwing out all my old papers and junk from school. For the life of me I couldn't remember why I hadn't just tossed the thing.

I slipped into bed and tried to make my mind a blank. I counted sheep and then switched to hockey balls banging off the backboards. Nothing worked. I thought back to the calendar remembering the star. *The star! That was it!* I sat up in bed, made my way over to my desk, and switched on the light. I rooted for the calendar and looked at it once again. The star might have originally signaled an exciting first day of camp day, but in the end it was more than that. It represented my ability to get through a tough year losing Mitch. I stared at it a long time wondering if I could get through losing Mitch a second time around 'cause I knew for sure, since he hadn't called, it probably already had happened.

After the blowup between Will and me, the atmosphere around the lunch table the next day was very subdued, everyone acting overly cautious as if the wrong thing were said or done, the whole world would end. I guessed the heated discussion between Will and me was more than enough drama for good digestion. It was going to be a long semester if I didn't do something to mend things, so I spoke up. "So, Will, you getting ready for basketball yet?"

It must have seemed like an olive branch had been thrown down on the table 'cause all of a sudden everyone started talking at once and Will gave me a lopsided grin, so maybe he was feeling a little awkward about yesterday, too. He started going into a long explanation about the conditioning he and the team were doing to get their season rolling, which wouldn't be for another two months, but I knew from the old talks I had with Mitch that basketball players were kind of year-round athletes. I wondered if Mitch would be part of that team since he was set to be a returning varsity player when he left last year, but I didn't dare ask.

* * *

It was Friday and the official opening of the hockey season. At lunch Will put his book down, and surveyed Sam, Anna, and me in our team shirts that we were wearing for our first home game. "What's up in girl-world?" he asked. "Since when can you all wear the same exact stuff to school and not get into some catfight?"

I saw the hint of a grin playing at the corners of his mouth as he waited for Anna's reaction. He was trying to flirt in his own brainiac way. Maybe she had put him in his place after his 'try playing an indoor sport' comment and now he was trying to get back in her good graces. I looked at Anna. Her eyes were shining. She combed her fingers through her long, black hair that she always wore down during school, and then she quickly gathered it up into a neat knot. Will couldn't take his eyes off her. *Way to work it Anna*, I thought. I was happy for them and wondered if something like that could ever come my way again.

By the time eighth period rolled around I was bouncing in my seat waiting for the game. As the bell rang I barely heard James wish me luck as I bolted toward the door.

The locker room was buzzing with game day preparations. Not only were we opening our season, girls' tennis and soccer were, too. If everyone in that locker room could have been plugged into an electric socket we could have energized every house in South Jersey.

When we got to the field our managers, Brit and Nadja, already had our pregame music blaring away, and, as we went through our warm-up drills, my feet felt as though they were skimming across the ground. Everything was easy and effortless. I couldn't wait to get to the cage and take some shots. There was something about hitting the ball and hearing it bang against the backboards that made my heart race.

Unfortunately my 'high' didn't last too long. As the game began it quickly seemed like I had been squeezed into a small box. Everywhere I went there was a defender stepping toward me blocking my chances to get the ball. I had faced tight marking last year as I started scoring a lot of goals, even some double-teaming, but this was different.

At the end of the half the score was still 0-0. We couldn't get the ball out of the midfield and I was getting frustrated.

"Look girls," Coach said patiently, "you're not seeing what's going on. Are they playing zone or man?" Her question was met by silence, one of those big 'please don't call on me' moments. Eyes were everywhere – on the ground, the horizon, the bleachers, everywhere but on Coach. And I totally got it 'cause I'd been there more times than I could count.

There was a ton of stuff I had to learn about hockey, but one thing I did know — no one was playing me man-to-man. "Zone," I said, breaking the silence.

"How do you know?" Coach asked.

"There isn't the same person staying with me when I cut … so I guess … process of elimination."

Coach smiled. "Good one, Jackie. You're right. They're playing zone, so this is what we're going to do …"

After she gave us some direction it got a lot easier. I got loose on a double cut with Sam and was able to get my stick on Kate's pass into the circle. The ball careened into the cage for a score. As I jogged back to the center of the field I smiled to myself. *Okay, Chris Hanson. That one is for you.*

The game ended with Jules taking a penalty stroke making the final score 2-0. We were pretty pumped afterwards. Even though the game had been harder than we had anticipated, it was one in the victory column and I'd take that any day.

(9)

Coach gave us Saturday off saying since we had worked so hard these last few weeks we probably needed to catch up on our school work. I overheard Kate tell Jess Piotrowski she thought the real reason we had off was because Coach and Ms. Gillespie were going to scout some Saturday morning games being played by our upcoming opponents. Whatever the reason, I knew it would be one of the few Saturdays I could sleep in.

It was nearly noon when I woke and an uneventful weekend stretched out before me. I tried to banish any thoughts of what Mitch might be doing now he was back in South Jersey. After finishing my Spanish homework and skimming through the latest topic in algebra, I soon became bored. I glanced at my mom's 'to do' list and knew I had little motivation to tackle anything there, so I decided to call the twins. Neither one picked up their cells. And then I remembered that Tori had her Saturday afternoon art class and probably had turned off her phone, but where was Jules?

My thumb started absently tapping against my cell phone. I needed something to do, somebody to call. I almost dropped the phone when it suddenly rang.

"Hello," I said hesitantly, not recognizing the number.

"Jackie, it's me, Cassie Henry. You know … from hockey."

"Oh yeah, sure." I started to open my bureau drawer trying to figure out my day and what I should wear.

"I know it's kind of late and don't know your plans, but I was wondering if you wanted to play some hockey. I really could use your help with some things. But if you're busy ..."

"No, no, that's okay," I said. She asked if she could bring her sister along who also played hockey, and within moments my mind was filling up with ideas on how I could help them. I was already rummaging through my sky-high pile of dirty clothes for something to wear before Cassie hung up.

I was halfway to the park when my bike started to wobble. Pulling over to a grassy strip along the road I noticed the cause as soon as I got off the bike. *A rear flat tire — rats!* I still had almost a mile to go. I debated bagging the whole afternoon and turning back like it was just one of those 'one-star' days you see in the horoscopes. One that basically tells you to stay in bed and wait for better days ahead, but I walked on knowing that Cassie and her sister were expecting me.

Just as I got to the park, I saw Cassie and her sister leaving the park on their bikes. I waved, "Hey, wait up."

Both girls stopped and Cassie said, "We thought you blew us off."

"No, no. My bike — see," I said, showing them my flat tire. "Come on. We can still play."

Cassie seemed relieved and introduced me to her sister who was on Northfield's freshman team. As we walked toward the park's playing field we talked about what they wanted to work on. In the beginning Cassie's sister was kind of nervous, so I told her about things that happened to me my freshman year — my worries over the cut list, she nodding on that one, and how long it had taken us to become a real team. Pretty soon she started to relax.

I spent over an hour working on their skills. It felt really good to see them making progress. During a break I asked Cassie about her old school in Tennessee. "It was so hard to leave," she said. "I ran track and miss my team a lot."

"She was district hurdles champion," her sister said proudly.

I thought it must be hard to start over after so much past success. I wondered if Mitch missed his Northfield buddies when he moved to Texas, and if so, if they were the only people he missed.

When we were finished playing, Cassie offered to call their dad and have him cart my bike home, but I said I was fine and needed the walk to cool down. I slung my stick bag over my shoulder and steered my bike toward the side of the road. After the first mile I cursed myself for not carrying a can of instant tire inflator and decided to add it to my 'to-do' list.

I hadn't gone too much further when I heard a car moving slowly behind me. I glanced over my shoulder to see a sleek, black Tahoe pulling over to the side of the road. As the car stopped, a big bear of a man stepped out and waved. It was Mitch Kennedy's dad.

My eyes glanced at the car wondering if Mitch was sitting there behind the darkened glass. I tried to smooth my hair just in case, but knew it was useless. I looked a mess.

"Hi, Major Kennedy," I said, praying that he was alone yet hoping he wasn't.

"Jackie, looks like you're having some trouble with your bike. How about I give you a hand?"

Not waiting for a reply, he loaded the bike into the back of his truck, and as I slid into the empty seat alongside of him, I felt both relief and disappointment.

"You should have a tire inflator with you when you ride," he said, shifting into gear and easing back onto the road.

"I know. I forgot," I said, thinking how silly I must seem to a former military man whose life had depended on always being prepared for anything.

He glanced at the net bag sitting at my feet that had a half dozen balls inside. "Getting in more practice I see. Team going to be good this year?"

"Hope so. We have a lot of returning players," I said, nervously turning my hockey stick in my hands wondering how long we would be driving before Mitch's name would come up. I searched my mind for something more to say. After an awkward moment or two I asked, "So how's your retirement going?" As soon as the words popped out of my mouth I wanted to reel them back in. I mean what girl asks her old boyfriend's dad a geeky question like that?

But I had to give Major Kennedy a mental fist bump 'cause he didn't laugh or roll his eyes. Instead he seemed to be considering my question seriously. "Actually, Jackie, I'm enjoying it more than I thought I would," he finally said. "I'm doing consulting work for a security firm in Philadelphia, and, of course, now that Mitch is back he's keeping me pretty busy."

Busy doing what? Is he happy to be here again? Why hasn't he called me? I silently hurled the questions at Mitch's dad only to feel the frustration of not having any answers.

We turned onto my street, and as if he could read my mind, he said, "Mitch was sure glad his mother decided to let come back to be with me to finish his schooling at Northfield. He had to start a few days late since the school seemed to have lost some of his paperwork.

I tried to be cool, nodding like, of course, happens all the time, yet as we got to my house, I already had my hand on the door handle, anxious to escape. Major Kennedy was a good guy, but it still felt awkward riding in the car with him knowing that his son probably liked someone else now, since he sure wasn't interested in me anymore.

As we pulled into the drive, the garage door opened and my dad came out, surprised to see who I was with. "Mike, good to see you. It's been a while," my dad said, as he shook hands with Mitch's dad. Then my dad turned to me and saw my messed up bike.

I tried to get past my dad's words …'it's been a while,' when I squeaked out a "Yeah, flat tire," and mumbled something about Major Kennedy coming to my rescue.

My dad pulled me into an embrace while he invited Mitch's dad in for coffee. For a moment it was freshman year all over again 'cause Mitch's dad and my parents had been pretty friendly and had even had occasional dinners together. That sure wouldn't be happening anymore.

Fortunately for me Major Kennedy begged off the coffee invite saying he had to get home. I thanked him for bailing me out, and as I went in the house I wondered if he would tell his son I had seen me. *Probably not.* I tried to swallow a gigantic lump that was starting to build in my throat as I raced up the stairs.

(10)

On the night before our first big out-of-conference game, Lizzie came prancing into my room like she had some whooping big secret, and flopped on my bed. "You should see what they're saying about your team," she said smugly.

I looked up from my English book. "What are you talking about?" I asked.

"It's on the Internet. A hockey forum. They say Park Ridge is going to kick your butts, and you'll be lucky to make states."

"First of all," I said, "you're not supposed to be on the Internet without Mom or Dad's permission. If they found out you were they'd kill you. And how did you get on a hockey forum anyway?" I asked, torn both with curiosity about what was on the forum, and concern for my sister surfing the Net on her own.

Lizzie could tell I was a little peeved, so she said more quietly, "A girl in fifth grade. We were talking at recess. She told me how to get on."

"Show me," I said, pulling her over to my desk.

A couple of clicks of my mouse, and she pulled up the site. *You little devil*, I thought. I looked over her shoulder as she scrolled through all the comments. "See," she said, obviously pleased with herself again.

My little sister was right. We were being slammed. At first I was so ticked off about what was being said about us that I forgot Lizzie's part in discovering the site. Then I thought of all the lectures I had gotten from Dad about all the crazies out in the world who tried to latch on to young unsuspecting kids, pretending to be someone they weren't, and knew I had to deal with my sister. I turned the chair around so she had to face me. "If you ever go on the Internet again without Mom or Dad saying it is okay I will make your life miserable. Do you understand?"

Her face crumpled and her eyes started to fill up. I bit my lip, but plowed ahead. "Not everyone on the Internet is who they say they are, and it's pretty hard to tell the good guys from the bad guys." I raised her chin and made her look me in the eye. "Promise me, okay?"

She nodded her head. I was pretty sure she meant it, so I gave her a hug. I had played the mean, big sister long enough. I honestly didn't know how anybody could become a parent and have to do all this scolding stuff, and decided then and there that maybe being single for the rest of my life, or at least not having children, was probably a good idea.

* * *

I was mighty excited as I dressed for the game the next morning. It was going to be fun to play a top school from the North. I surveyed myself in the mirror, turning this way and that, making sure my navy kilt and white home shirt looked perfect.

Mom dropped me and the twins off at school around eleven for our twelve o'clock game. Once we were out of the car I let the twins know what Lizzie had discovered on the

Internet. By the time we were through the pre-game warmup the whole team knew, and they were steamed. Some said they were going to get on the forum as soon as they got home, and try to figure where the comments were coming from.

We went through the first half like we were playing the 'slams' on the forum instead of our real live opponents on the field. The other team was totally beating us to the ball, and if it wasn't for Becky's heroic saves we would have been down by a bunch of goals.

I could tell halftime was going to be ugly. I looked at Mrs. Fortunata and her face was kind of turning purple like she was holding her breath and trying to count to a hundred before she'd say anything she'd regret later.

The huddle was silent for the longest time. Players didn't even pass the water bottles around because they were so afraid of what Coach would say. Finally Becky spoke up. "Coach, you just gotta breathe." We all flicked our eyes wildly toward Becky and cringed, wondering if she had just sent Coach over the top and now we'd all pay.

Instead we heard laughter as Coach put her hand over her eyes and shook her head back and forth. Then she rubbed the back of her neck and said, "What am I going to do with you girls?"

Since there wasn't going to be any answer for that she got serious. "You're playing like your heads are someplace else." We could have told her why we weren't focused, but didn't think she wanted to hear our excuses. So, after a brief moment, she continued. "You need to start acting as one giant force. Like a tidal wave that keeps rolling at them for the next twenty-five minutes. Can you do that?"

We nodded. We got it. The picture of an enormous wave was such a perfect description of how we should act.

We went out on the field with our heads in the game. We held Park Ridge and were eventually able to score a goal on our own. We had escaped and I hoped we had learned a valuable lesson about outside distractions. Then I overheard Lindsay saying she was going to post our score on the forum and see what reaction it would get. It was going to be a long season.

*   *   *

The next week we pulled off two more wins. Like last year, I was the team's leading scorer, and was starting to get mail from colleges every couple of days. I'd look at the name of the school, shaking my head in amazement. I couldn't even drive a car yet, and people were writing me from schools that weren't even in New Jersey. Something was seriously wrong with that. I was starting to accumulate a huge pile in the back of my closet where I stashed the college mail. I knew better than to toss them out remembering how stupid I was deleting all the coaches' emails, but figured I wouldn't have to think about them 'til next fall.

My dad soon put a stop to my stockpiling one night after dinner."Jackie, your mom was cleaning out closets to make room for winter clothes and said she discovered a pile of college mail. Think we should talk about this?"

Rats! I groaned. "It's nothing, Dad. Schools probably send stuff to everybody," I said, trying to be all nonchalant so my dad would drop it. I should have known better. My dad wasn't a special investigator for the United States Postal Department for nothing. My brother and I found out long ago that while he hunted out the bad guys during the daytime, his night job was to investigate everything about us kids. So he wasn't going to be put off by my 'it's nothing comment' at all.

My dad leaned back in his dining room chair and folded his arms across his chest.

"Why don't you show me what you've got?" he said.

I grudgingly rolled out of my chair like Dad was sending me to the guillotine. I **so** didn't want to deal with this stuff. When I plopped the pile of envelopes onto the dining room table Dad's eyes lit up in surprise.

He rifled through the envelopes and his eyes caught sight of the postmark of a couple of the first ones I got. He pulled them out of the pile. "You've had these two awhile. When were you going to open them?"

I wriggled around in my chair. 'Never' probably wasn't the answer he was looking for. I huffed, "It's only my junior year."

"You're right. You're only a junior and it'll be a long time before you go to college." He started flipping through the pile again and then he said, "You don't have to go to a four-year school, anyway. There's always community college. And besides, no one says you have to keep playing hockey."

Community college! What? And no hockey? I wasn't liking where this conversation was going. It was as though someone was closing doors on my future. Then a light bulb flickered on and I realized that someone was me. I slinked down in my chair. I wasn't happy. I really didn't want to deal with this college stuff, but I didn't want anybody telling me no more hockey either.

(11)

After the 'college thing' bounced back and forth between my dad and me, we arrived at a compromise. I would open each letter, read what the coach had to say, and then I would file it. Dad even went out and bought me a file folder, one that was alphabetized so I could keep things super organized. He said I didn't have to write back just yet, but I still thought he was pushing it.

The only thing that made me agree to any of it was, okay, it was two things — it was my dad I was talking to, not exactly a person I could say 'no' to, and more importantly, the picture I had floating in my head of a big sign of a hockey stick with a diagonal line going through it.

After practice the next afternoon, as we were waiting for the late buses, Jules was in a talking mood which kind of surprised me since it had seemed all about her and Kate for weeks. She asked if I had heard from any colleges. I told her a few, so I, of course, had to be polite and ask her the same.

"Yeah, there are a bunch I'm really excited about," she said. "I heard from a couple of schools in California even. Mom and I are flying out for some 'un-officials' after Thanksgiving."

I didn't even know what an 'un-official' was, or an 'official' for that matter, but I tried to be cool and asked her more about the schools. She was really into it. Like she knew she wanted pre-law, and was interested in entertainment law because of all of her discussions with James about copywriting and intellectual property rights for musicians and stuff. She was hoping if she liked any of the schools they might give her money for playing hockey and, of course, for academics. "A lot depends on how well I do on my SATs which I'll take in November and then maybe again in January," she said.

"Holy cow, Jules," I said. "Don't you think you ought to just chill and enjoy life?"

She gave me a funny look. "I **am** enjoying it. It's just that Kate said you can never start too soon."

I frowned at the mention of Kate. "Well as long as Kate said it, I guess that makes it perfect," I said, turning away, and walking toward the late bus that was pulling up to the curb. I really had enough.

*   *   *

I didn't play so hot in the next game, probably 'cause I was too focused on the chumminess between Jules and Kate. I must have missed half the balls that came to me and watched so many trickle over the sideline or go to the other team that I lost count. I couldn't talk to Tori about it 'cause, for one, it was about Jules, and two, Tori was so wrapped up in the progress she was making with the cutie in her chemistry class she barely knew I was alive.

To make matters worse, that night my mom decided to start hammering me about **my** 'to-do' list that was still taped on my bedroom mirror. I snapped, "It isn't my list. It's yours. Besides I have all of junior year to work on it." It mustn't have sat to well with her 'cause she told me I was grounded for the weekend. So, I stamped my way up to my room. I knew my punishment was no big deal since I wasn't having much of a social life anyway, but my mom didn't need to know that.

I tried to catch up on some school work, and must have read one page of *A Lesson Before Dying* fifty times. Finally I gave up. I looked across the room to the annoying piece of paper still taped to my mirror. *How did I get into this mess? I haven't been grounded since seventh grade when I forgot to call Mom and Dad to tell them I was at the movies with the twins.* I got off the bed and wandered over to the bureau to get a closer look at the list.

I thought about my dad's warning — no college, no hockey. *Maybe I should take the SATs, maybe I should try to be a little smarter so I could go to college.* I went downstairs and found my mom in the laundry room folding my newly washed uniform which made me feel even more guilty for being such a crummy daughter.

Closing the gap between us, I rested my elbows on the dryer and watched her work. She didn't acknowledge my presence, but kept on sorting the clothes. "I'm sorry," I said quietly. She looked up. "Really," I said.

She put down the socks she was matching up. "What's the matter with you today?"

"I don't know." My eyes started to get a little teary. "Nothing feels right. I can't explain it."

She reached for me and pulled me close. "Oh, Jackie, nothing is easy about growing up. But you can't take it out on other people."

I nodded my head against her cheek. "I'm going to work on my vocabulary list for the SATs and I'll check with my guidance counselor about the SAT classes. Okay?"

"That's a good start, honey. And I'll do something for you. I know part-time jobs are hard to come by, especially in this economy, but you might want to try The Grand, the movie house over in Voorhees. I saw Mr. Halscheid, the owner, at the cleaners today," she said, "and he was complaining that two of his employees just quit for jobs at the mall."

I brightened. *A movie theater! I like to go to movies. How hard would it be to take tickets? I know how to sweep floors and clean up, my own room being the exception, of course.*

"I'll drive you over tomorrow afternoon to get an application," Mom said. "You're still grounded for the rest of the weekend, though." I nodded. I could live with it. I ran back up the stairs feeling a heck of a lot better than I did an hour ago.

*   *   *

At lunch the following Monday, I was telling Anna all about my good chances on scoring a job at The Grand, especially after my mom chatted up the owner while I was filling out the application. Then Noah and his girlfriend arrived at the table. "Hey guess what?" Noah said excitedly, dropping his books on the table. "We've made a video of that song." He looked at me. "You know, *A Moment Ago.*"

I felt the color drain from my face. It was my song. At least the words were. I had written it for an English assignment right after Mitch left school. James, who had been in my English class last year, too, had done a bit of editing and had put some music to it, and now it was part of the band's regular set. The thing was, nobody around school, except for the band, knew the words were mine.

"What song is that?" Anna asked.

Noah took one look at my face and said, "Oh it's just a song James worked on. Anyway, people seem to like it a lot so the band decided to use it to help us get more exposure. It's on YouTube. You gotta check it out."

Everyone at the table started pumping Noah with questions. This was big news for anyone at Northfield, and they understood how people got pretty famous sometimes when **an** Internet video got a lot of action. "We need a ton of hits for everyone to take us seriously," Noah said. So everyone sat there strategizing how they could let their friends know about it. Not just the kids from Northfield either, but people they knew from other schools, too.

"Hey, we could even 'like' it on our Facebook page, Anna said. "If the video takes off, it could reach thousands. I kept my tongue as the others got caught up in the excitement. A ton of strangers could hear how much I was hurting when Mitch left and I wasn't sure I liked that idea very much at all.

*   *   *

My English teacher, Mrs. North, was piling on the vocabulary words. I barely got their spelling right half the time let alone remembered their meanings. One afternoon we had a sub and she was pretty much letting us do anything we wanted. I remembered the SAT promise to my mom so I asked James, "How come you're doing so well on your vocab quizzes?"

"I read a lot," he said, "plus I try to use the words every day. Look at today's list."

The first word was — *Accelerate*: To go faster. "Okay," he said, "apply it to hockey."

"That's easy. You should always accelerate after you dodge an opponent."

"Right. Try the next one."

The word was adroit which meant having skills in the use of bodily or mental powers. I thought for a moment, then said, "She was adroit at weaving through small spaces while keeping the ball on her stick."

James fist bumped me. "You got it."

I beamed. Using all the words like I was in a hockey game made it a heck of a lot easier. *I might even try some words on Jules — might even stump her. Maybe when I get home today I might be able to cross one item off my 'to-do' list.*

Before practice I tried to impress Jules with my new vocabulary. She grinned and then showed me her advanced placement word lists. They might as well have been the vocabulary lists for her Spanish Four class. That's how clueless I was looking down the lists of words. I guessed the cross-out on my 'to do' list was going to have to be postponed.

*   *   *

That week we had three more wins. We were on a roll at 9-0 and I wondered if there was any stopping us. And then on Monday something sure stopped me. My algebra teacher asked me to drop a note at the main office before I went to my next class. He gave me a late pass in case I didn't get to my next class on time, which was gym. I dropped off the note and started to make my way down a different hallway on my way to the gym. It was then that I saw Mitch again. He was talking to some girl, and as she leaned up to whisper something in his ear she wrapped her arm around his neck like she owned him. It was then that I realized the girl was Emma Connors.

Mitch half turned toward her. In my hurry to escape I bumped into some big kid, which caused the boy behind me to crash into me. All of a sudden I was in the middle of some chain-reaction multi-student pile-up. I regained my balance amidst a bunch of curses, and 'why don't you look where you're going' comments. I strained to look back over the taller kids to see if Mitch was still there, but he wasn't, and neither was Emma.

I ducked and weaved my way through the congestion, and took off down another hallway. I needed time to breathe and knew I couldn't face Emma just then knowing what I just saw. Ten minutes later I got to the safety of an empty locker room and collapsed down on the bench by my locker. This was the 'worst of worsts.' Emma had obviously finally gotten her hooks into Mitch. My world was ending.

Mrs. Fortunata was walking through the locker room when she spied me sitting there. "Jackie, don't you have gym now?"

"Oh, yeah." I waved my late pass. "I was doing an errand for Mr. Hoffner."

"You better hurry or you'll miss the whole class." She stood in the middle of the locker room with her hands on her hips and seemed to be debating whether to move on to her office or continue the conversation.

I made an attempt to spin the locker combination to get out my stuff for class. The numbers were so blurry it took three tries 'til it finally opened. I half turned to find Coach sitting on the bench just a few feet away.

"Do you want to talk?" Mrs. Fortunata said in a voice softer than I ever heard her use before.

I couldn't bring myself to look at her. I just shook my head no. She hesitated, then said, "I'm always here if you need me." I heard her get up and walk away. I quickly reached into my locker for my shorts and T-shirt, changed, and hurried out to the field.

That afternoon we had another game, and as I stepped onto the field for our pregame warmup, I resolved that winning a state championship couldn't be simply some nice goal. My heart hardened. It was something that had to happen.

Going through our stick drills I noticed the stands were quickly filling up. Fans were even beginning to line up along the roped-off area that stretched from one end of the field to the other. A few of the Northfield parents looked like proud peacocks wearing their *'We are Northfield Hockey'* sweatshirts or jackets in our school colors, shaking each others' hands and clapping each other on the back, like they were the ones on the team, and had already won the game.

Lindsay pointed to them and said, "Hey, we've got quite a fan club. Bet they can't wait to see us win number ten."

I thought she was being a little cocky, but then I heard Kate say, "Yeah, this'll be an easy one."

I frowned. Was everyone thinking we had a lock on the season? I noticed some others joking around, and I guess Coach saw it too 'cause she jumped all over us in our pregame huddle. And for the first time I could remember, the players didn't really pay attention to anything she had to say.

Our opponent was New Gretna whose record was 5-5. Knowing this, even I didn't think they'd give us much trouble. The game started with us rushing toward their goal cage almost as soon as the whistle blew, but their defense was able to hold us off and deflect our first series of shots.

Maybe we got to their goal area too easily, and just thought the rest of the game would go our way, or maybe they gained confidence when we didn't score right away. Whatever the reason, as the game went on we stopped being aggressive, and sat back on our heels waiting for them to give us an opportunity to just walk the ball into the cage, just because we were Northfield hockey.

Coach went crazy at halftime. She didn't even try to hold her breath. She just let us have it. But it was too late. We had dug our own grave, and couldn't seem to find a way out of it. We lost 0-1 on a quick move by an unmarked player right in front of Becky's pads. Afterwards it was quiet in the huddle. Coach didn't say too much to us. I don't even know what she could have said. You could barely hear our cheer for the other team. We were pathetic. To add to our wounds as we were walking off the field, we overheard some of our own parents talking about how we blew the whole season. It seemed like some of them thought it was their season instead of ours.

The next morning's sports page said it all. Under the high school sports section was the headline —

New Gretna Delivers Fatal Blow to Undefeated Northfield

That our loss was a headline was bad enough, but the word fatal played itself over and over in my head and I bet it did for my teammates, too.

When I opened my hall locker, a piece of paper floated to the floor. I stooped to pick it up It said —

Tough loss – sorry!

I looked around the hallway trying to figure out who might have stuffed it in my locker. *Somebody from JV or maybe someone from the band? Whoever you are you got that right,* I thought, wondering again who wrote it.

Somehow it was reassuring to know there was someone out there who had my back and at least took the trouble to write a note.

That afternoon everybody was taking their time dressing for practice. Each of us had a pretty good idea what was facing us when we got to the field. Coach was going to sprint us to death and we deserved it.

Coach surprised us though. She had us sit in the bleachers instead. "Girls, yesterday we were getting caught up in being undefeated," she said, as she took her time making eye contact with each of us. "We've been getting good crowds because we've been winning, and sometimes people along the sidelines assume we're going to keep on winning. That can be a distraction, and sometimes we start believing what we hear other people say." She slipped her hands into her jacket pocket and paced around a bit like she was collecting her thoughts. Then she turned to face us, her voice very quiet. "Nobody is declared a winner until the final whistle. The minute we think otherwise we don't honor our opponent, honor ourselves, or honor the game."

After Coach was finished speaking there was an uneasy silence. We knew we had let our coach down, and ourselves, too. Then Jules stood, "We apologize, Coach. Everything you said was right. Kate and I didn't do our job either 'cause we didn't see it coming.

I sucked in my breath. Jules was putting too much on herself. Besides, if anybody was acting blasé it was Kate, not Jules. I stood up. "No, it was all of us. We're all responsible for what happened. We just have to make sure it doesn't happen again." Jules met my eyes, and I knew she was grateful. For a moment it was the same old connection that had always existed between Jules and me. Maybe it was time for a talk.

(12)

That night I slipped in my ear buds and tried to drown out the week with some sweet music from Casey Collins. After a while even my favorite band couldn't help with the thoughts banging around inside my head. Part of it was about Mitch coming back to Northfield, and maybe thinking, from what Will inferred at least, that I had forgotten all about him, and had taken up with the twins' brother. I had no way of telling him it wasn't like that, and besides it was probably too late since it looked like Emma Connors had finally gotten her claws into him. Like if it was some nice girl, one that deserved him, maybe it wouldn't be so bad. But who was I kidding? I wanted him for myself, and that was all there was to it.

Then there was the whole thing with Jules, our friendship being one messed up thing. It was all enough to make me want to skip junior year entirely. Then I got to thinking about all the good times Jules and I had on the field together. That's when I yanked off my ear buds and grabbed the phone. When Jules answered before I had time to think, I blurted out, "I've been a jerk and miss us being best buddies."

"What's going on, Jackie?"

I started pacing around the room. I didn't know how to answer her. I wanted to say, *I should be your friend, not*

Kate. But the idea sounded so elementary school. Suddenly I stopped my pacing. Jules hadn't said she missed me too.

I froze up. "I don't know what's going on. Forget it." The conversation wasn't going the way I pictured it. "I guess I just wanted to say hi, that's all," I said, not being able to think of anything else.

"Okay, well ... see you at practice, I guess."

She disconnected and I sat down on the edge of the bed with my phone in my hand wondering what the heck had happened, and if I lost my friend for good.

*   *   *

The next day we had an away game. Sitting in the back of the bus with Anna I found myself looking up to the front of the bus catching Jules and Kate in conversation with Coach. I felt miserable.

I felt a tug on my arm. "What's the matter? You seem so far away," Anna said.

I smiled. She was right. I was far away thinking about all the years it had been Jules, Tori, and me, the three musketeers. I thought it would always be that way. Looking at Anna I remembered back two years when we were freshmen, and how it was she who had walked away from some of her eighth grade friends to come over to our lunch table and introduce herself to us. At the time I thought it was such a brave thing to do. I still did.

"Sorry about the squabble with Will the other day. You like him, right?" I said.

"Major crush for two years. Ever since ninth grade algebra," she said, blushing. "I couldn't believe it when he walked me from class to lunch and then sat down at the same table with me. He had barely ever said two words to me."

"I think he's pretty shy when it comes to girls. Has he asked you out yet?"

"I think he's working up to it. You know 'what do I like to do on weekends kind of thing.' I didn't realize he was so close to Mitch Kennedy. Your old boyfriend, right?"

Before I could answer, Coach called from the front of the bus, "Jackie come on up."

Surprised, I slid past Anna and made my way toward the front as Kate and Jules vacated the seat next to Coach and began to make their way to the back. "Oh, you're in trouble," Kate said, laughing playfully. I felt my hands curl up into fists. I so wanted to punch her. I glanced quickly at Jules, but she simply slipped by me.

As I took a seat across from Coach I mentally reviewed the last few days of practice trying to figure out what I had done wrong and couldn't come up with a thing.

"Jackie, I've been meaning to talk to you," Coach said. "A friend of mine told me she emailed you after seeing you play at the invitational tournament this summer, and she hadn't heard back from you. Does that mean you're not interest in her school?"

I fingered the hem of my kilt picking at a loose thread. How could I tell her that I thought all those emails were someone's idea of being funny? She seemed to be waiting for me to speak. I had to accept the fact that she'd know I was an idiot. "I thought your friend's email, and all the others people sent were like a joke someone was playing on me, so I deleted them," I said.

I scrunched up my shoulders waiting for her to laugh, or yell, or something. Instead she pinched the bridge of her nose, and then kneaded her forehead like she was getting a migraine. I was thinking maybe she couldn't believe I was on her team, and wasn't some elementary school kid who had snuck up to eleventh grade like a stowaway on a plane. Finally she looked me. "Sorry," I whispered and felt a lump forming in my throat.

I watched her lean back in her seat and close her eyes for a moment. Then she let out a sigh. "My fault, Jackie. I should have prepared you for this. I assumed since your parents had been through the recruiting routine for soccer with your brother they would have talked to you already."

"Well, Dad did tell me I had to stop tossing college stuff in the back of my closet. He bought me a file and said I had to get organized. I never told him about the emails, though."

Coach smiled. "What's done is done. I'll tell my friend to contact you again, but this time, don't delete the email right away. Okay?" I nodded, relieved I could start breathing once again and maybe Coach didn't think I was the biggest loser ever.

"Have you written back to any of the schools yet?"

I shook my head. "I haven't done anything. To be honest ... I don't think I'm ready to think about college."

"You may not be ready to make a final decision, but you do need to look at what's out there. Unfortunately college coaches are filling out their future rosters earlier and earlier. Some players are making a commitment to a school when they're only fifteen."

Fifteen! My eyes bugged out of my head. I started to shrink away from Coach. It was all too much.

"Look at it this way," Coach said. "You want to watch some TV when you get home from school, but you have schoolwork first. So what do you do? You check the listings for what's on that night and DVR something you want to watch when you have your homework done, right."

"Yeah, I guess," I said, sensing where she was starting to go.

"Call it preparation for later. Just get as much information as you need right now and you can sort it out when you're ready. So do me favor, look through the pamphlets, and send a note to those that seem interesting. I'll write you a sample note if you need help. What do you say?"

"Sounds like one of my dumb algebra equations," I grumbled.

Coached raised her eyebrows.

"You know, like doing a whole lot of steps just to get to the answer."

She laughed. "I guess it does. But if you do each step right you get a better ending."

"Okay, I'll do it," I said reluctantly.

She let out a breath when I said this. I guessed sometimes us players could make a coach really age when we were being so goofy about a whole bunch of different things.

*   *   *

Friday was another away conference game and if we won, we'd be in at least a tie for first place in our Mid-American North Conference. At lunch Sam, Anna, and I were pumped talking about the game. We remembered the team from last year. They had a great goalkeeper, probably the best in our conference outside of Becky, and we knew it would be a low-scoring game.

Will, who by now had changed his seat, was sitting next to Anna with his arm on the back of her chair, said to Noah, "I was thinking I might go to the game since there's no basketball practice today with the gym closed for a blood drive. Wanna go?"

Noah looked at his girlfriend and she nodded a yes. "I'll text James," Noah said. "He hardly ever gets to see Jules play between the band and his piano lessons.

The mention of Jules' name made me feel a little sad, that, and the fact that nobody was coming to see me play. Dad was busy with a big mail fraud case, and Mom, of course, with her substitute teaching, had wanted to be home in the afternoons to get stuff done around the house. I was happy for Anna that Will, at least an inch at a time, seemed to be working his way toward making her his girl, but ... I quietly gave myself a pinch. I needed to end my little pity party.

When we got to the field I was surprised to see an enormous crowd gathering 'cause it wasn't like it was a title game or state tournament contest. Maybe it was the weather. Despite it being the middle of October, it felt more like the end of summer. Everyone was in their shirtsleeves enjoying the last rays of the warm sun. It was a great day for hockey.

We were **so on** in our warm-up. Everybody looked good. I thought the game would be a perfect ending to the school week. In the huddle Tori whispered to me, "Our dad is here."

I looked at her with concern. Most kids would be pretty happy if one of their parents came to a game, but I was one of the few people who knew the twins wanted their dad to stay away from their sports stuff. He was such a perfectionist, that the twins, despite being so tall, had long ago made the decision not to play basketball. They had also pushed to go to a public school so they wouldn't have their dad, who was the boys' basketball coach at St. Benedict's, looking over their shoulders. Of course their brother, Chris, hadn't escaped, and he wound up playing for his dad. How he put up with it I didn't know. It wasn't like Mr. Hanson couldn't be a good guy and he'd always been nice to me. I just would never want to be coached by him.

"Did you know your dad was coming?" I asked. Tori shook her head, and I gave her hand a squeeze. "It'll be okay," I whispered back. She rolled her eyes, and the whistle blew to get out on the field. The game was about to start.

The play was wide open. Passes were crisp and right on the money. I was feeling good. We hit their goalie with a barrage of shots, and to no one's surprise they were all turned away. This time, because we knew it would be hard to score, we were patient. We didn't panic and kept to our game plan of good ball possession. Toward the end of the half the other team's defense was starting to tire and make mistakes. I got a sweet pass from Lindsay, and took off down the field. There was only one defender left, and I beat her with a little stutter move. Their goalie came out on me to cut down my angle to shoot, so I sent a little reverse pass to Tori.

With the goalie gone, the cage was empty. All Tori had to do was walk the ball in. Instead, she missed it. The ball rolled harmlessly out of bounds, and the half was over.

In the halftime huddle Tori looked crushed. I patted her on the back. "Happens all the time, don't worry about it," I said.

In the second half, Tori might as well have not been on the field. It was the worst I had ever seen her play. Finally Coach had to sub her with one of the sophomores. I felt bad, so I redoubled my efforts to try to score, but just couldn't get around this goalkeeper. I was beginning to think she was working a voodoo charm on me or something. Just as the game was about to end in a scoreless tie Sam sent a rocket shot and the goalie had to dive on the ball. I was right there to put it in. The goalie knew she was in trouble so she deliberately kept the ball hidden under her outstretched glove. The whistle blew. I knew it was going to be a penalty stroke, a one on one with the goalkeeper.

Jules was our number one stroker. When she came to the line to take the stroke I knew she meant business. The umpire blew her whistle and the ball soared into the cage for a score. Two minutes later the game was over.

Our friends came up to the roped-off area that separated the team benches from the spectators and offered their congratulations. James gave Jules a hug and told her he was proud of her, and then Noah high-fived her. Further down the line I saw Will deep in conversation with Anna and thought maybe she was blushing. It looked like things were progressing nicely for them. I hoped so. I had to be honest though. It made me remember all the times Mitch had come to my games freshman year, and it made me miss him even more.

After the JV game was over I walked with the twins to their car as it was their turn to carpool. Tori was still upset about her play and Jules was trying to console her. I wasn't looking forward to the ride home if Mr. Hanson was going to say anything to make Tori feel any worse than she already did.

The twins asked me to sit in front with their father so they could keep some distance from any potential "feedback." We drove in silence, and I thought it was going to be okay. Then as we neared our town of Cumberland's Crossing, Mr. Hanson said, "Nice goal, Jules. Too bad you couldn't have one yourself, Tori."

I heard an intake of breath from the back and didn't know if it came from Tori or Jules. I searched for something to say, some change of subject to lighten up the moment. "Mr. Hanson, how's the basketball team going to be this year?" He flashed me a grin, and started telling me about their potential to reach the non-public school championship. As he buzzed away I wondered why he had to make everything so competitive, and hoped that Tori could let her dad's remarks roll off her back.

(13)

Saturday morning Coach scheduled a practice and when my mom pulled up at the twins' front door, only Jules came out. "Where's Tori? She sick?" I called to Jules as she approached our car.

Jules shook her head and slid into the back seat. "She's not coming."

I turned around in my seat expecting a further explanation, but Jules shook her head and mouthed "later." I watched my mom busying herself switching channels on the radio. Sometimes my mom could actually be cool and knew when not to butt in.

As we crossed the parking lot to the field Jules said, "We had a big row last night. Mom, Dad, Tori, and me. It was a mess. The bottom line is Mom's grounded Dad from coming to any more games and Tori's quitting hockey.

"What? She can't quit."

"Well she is. Tori pretends she doesn't care all that much about sports. She figures if she treats it all like it's just fun and games, she can't get her feelings hurt if she doesn't measure up. But it does matter to her and Dad took it over the top yesterday."

"What are you going to tell Coach?" I asked, as I hurried to catch up with Jules' long strides.

"I don't know. I don't want to lie."

"Why don't you tell her it's something personal, which it is, and Tori will come and talk to her about it on Monday."

Jules stopped in mid-stride, and turned to face me. "Good idea. Thanks, Jack. Maybe I can talk her back into it by then."

I almost brought up our own problems right then when Jules seemed so open, but I didn't. Instead I said, "Do you want me to try and talk with her?"

"Can't hurt," she said, as she walked away to talk to Coach. I was dumfounded. I thought I knew Tori, and then this happened. I shoved my feet into my cleats. How could we win without Tori? I mean, yeah, maybe she didn't have to be on the top of her game for us to win, but we needed her just the same. Besides, it wouldn't be as much fun without her.

* * *

On Sunday afternoon I called Tori. "Come play some tennis with me," I said. "We haven't done anything together since forever." Eventually, after some more persuasion, she agreed to meet me at the park.

"You're not going to try and talk me into anything are you," she asked suspiciously when we walked onto the tennis courts.

I grabbed my can of new tennis balls and popped off the lid trying to think of how to answer her. "I'd never try to force you into something you didn't really want," I said finally, hoping my answer was truthful enough.

After three sets of tennis where more balls flew over the fence or onto the other courts than ones landing over the net, we finally stopped, breathless and laughing. "I guess I won't be challenging for Northfield's number one singles position this year," I said between gulps of water.

Tori laughed, then grabbed my water bottle and poured the rest over her head. "Boy it's hot for this time of year. I can't believe it's only supposed to be in the fifties by Tuesday." Then she saw the serious look on my face. "You promised. No talking me into anything," she said.

I sat down by the fence and started to stretch. "Look …," I began, and Tori started to pace. "I know what I promised, but give me one little chance. I know you're upset about not making the goal, and yes, it would have been an easy one. But maybe it was too easy."

She stopped her pacing. "What do you mean too easy?"

"Remember in lacrosse last spring when the goalie clunked me on the head, and I got an eight meter shot?" Tori shrugged. "Well, anyway, the ref put the goalie behind me. There was no one in the cage. It was a no-brainer. I stood there and kept saying to myself, take your time. You've got a whole open cage. And you know what? I missed."

"Yeah, but we were beginners in lacrosse. I've been playing hockey a long time," Tori said.

I bet people who've been playing a long time, even longer than us, miss too," I said, as I stood up and leaned against the fence to stretch out my calves.

Tori finally started to stretch, too. "I know you're right," she said. "I guess I shouldn't get so hung up about it, but my dad is such a pain."

I had no answer for that. Her dad was a pain when it came to sports. "How did Chris do it, putting up with him for four years of basketball at St. Benedict's?"

Tori laughed. "You only think you know my brother. Chris doesn't say much, but he's pretty tough inside. From the time he was little, Chris seemed to be able to handle whatever Dad threw at him.

Tori was silent for a minute seeming to be thinking about stuff, so I didn't say anything as I grabbed my sneaker and pulled my leg back to stretch out my quads.

Finally, Tori started to do the stretch with me. "Remember when I told you a long time ago that Dad blew out his knee playing basketball in Italy?"

"Yeah, and that's where he met your mom."

She nodded. "Well, Mom told me once he couldn't play basketball anymore, he felt he had nothing. No pro career. No NBA. It really tore him up." Tori switched to the other leg. "Anyway what Chris realized, I guess, is that's why Dad pushes us so. He wants us to have what he couldn't."

To play in the NBA?" I asked puzzled.

Tori laughed and gave me a playful shove. She could tell I was really dense when it came to following a story. "No, goofy. Well, at least not Jules and me. He just wants us to be the best at everything. For a long time Chris went along with it to make Dad happy, at least until he picked a college."

I raised my eyebrows when she said that. I was kind of surprised at Chris' choice, too, 'cause it wasn't some big time basketball factory and Chris was really good.

"He told Dad he wanted to be a doctor and the college he would choose had to have a strong science program. I mean he still wanted to play basketball, but academics were the big thing."

"What did your dad say?"

"He was upset at first, but after a while he came around. I think Mom had a lot to do with it."

As we grabbed our bikes and started heading out of the park I tried to digest everything that Tori had said. I looked over at Tori as we hit the main road. "Do you think you could look at your dad the way Chris does?"

"I don't know," Tori said, and then changed the subject. "You know I miss not having lunch with you or doing anything together.

"Me, too.

"You and Jules gotta work out what's ever the matter between the two of you. Okay?"

It was the first time Tori had alluded to a change in our friendships. I didn't say anything, but knew she was right. I just needed to figure out how to get over the bump that seemed to be there, one that sometimes seemed more like a mountain. We parted after a mile and as I got to the place where I had met up with Mitch's dad, I tried to clear my head of all my mixed up feelings about Mitch coming back to Northfield. As I pedaled down the road I thought to myself, *keep it happy, keep it happy.* So I pictured a big white envelope with fancy letters scrawled across reading Dr. and Mrs. Christopher Hanson. It made me smile all the way home.

*   *   *

"What's going on with Tori?" Sam asked me at lunch. "Somebody in my English class said she wasn't playing anymore."

Anna stopped making goo-goo eyes at Will, and asked, "That's not true, is it?"

I took my time twirling spaghetti round and round onto my fork. I hated how rumors were always flying around at our school. If three people knew something first period, five hundred would find out about it by the end of the day. "I do know Jules told Coach at Saturday's practice that Tori's reason for not being there was personal," I finally said, not looking at either Anna or Sam as I answered.

I suspected neither of them thought that this was all I knew, but fortunately they let it go as Noah arrived at the table all excited and said, "Hey, you're all invited."

"What? To your wedding?" Sam asked.

"Pleeeeze. To our band's newest gig."

Suddenly hockey was forgotten. Everyone wanted to know where. And for myself, I had played the lonely single long enough. I needed to get out. Noah told us they would be playing at a battle of the bands. This one was on Longstreet Pier in Philly. "It's on the last Saturday in October, their big final weekend before the close for winter renovations," he said. "The 'under twenty-one bands,' like us, have got from two 'til six and then at eight the 'over twenty-ones' go on. We need to get as big a crowd as possible. Everyone in the audience gets to vote."

What's the winner get," I asked.

"Seven hundred and fifty dollars, but more importantly an audition with Dick Hendricks Productions," Noah said. He could see we were clueless so he added, "He's the biggest promoter of new talent in the entire Delaware Valley. If he likes you, it opens a lot of doors."

"How are the YouTube hits coming?" I asked, hoping in a twisted way that people weren't all that interested in listening to the song.

"Great. Jules had her brother get his college buddies to listen to it so now we're getting a lot more hits."

"Terrific, just what I need, more and more people hearing my thoughts about Mitch. I noticed with the mention of Jules' brother Will's interest in the conversation seemed to disappear as he groped under his chair for an always present paperback book soon losing himself in some sci-fi story. Thinking about the time I wrote the song I felt the muscles in my neck start to tighten and felt a headache coming on.

In English, James wasn't quite as enthusiastic as Noah about the battle of the bands. "Noah's really pushing for this. I'm not sure it's the right thing for us, though," he said, as he pulled his homework out of his satchel.

"Why not? Noah said you could get a tryout with some big production company."

He grabbed the pencil tucked behind his ear and began doodling on a piece of scrap paper. "Here's the thing. The battle of the bands usually winds up about being who can sing the most popular songs the loudest. I mean, don't get me wrong, the crowds know if you suck, but I'm not sure we're a big-sound kind of band."

I guessed being in a band was kind of like being on a team. Eventually everyone needed to be on the same page for things to work. I studied the knot of concentration that had formed on James' brow and wondered what that meant for the future of the band.

*   *   *

When I walked into the locker room it was already buzzing with rumors. "Tori's in there talking to Coach now." "What's going to happen?" "Will Jules' quit if Tori gets kicked off?" Curiosity and tension were swirling all around me, and, as I changed, I caught furtive glances pointed in my direction, but I kept on dressing pretending I didn't notice.

Someone turned to Kate. "You ought to know what's going on." From the deer in the headlights look on Kate's face she was clearly uncomfortable with all of the buzz.

Finally I stood on the bench and yelled, "We better get to the field. We have five minutes 'til practice starts." That got everyone moving. As I hurried out to the field it struck me that people liked to be on-lookers to someone else's drama, but when it came to action they were pretty much happy not to be involved. I just hoped whatever was going on in Coach's office it would work out for Tori. If she didn't play anymore I would miss her terribly.

Ms. Gillespie was already at the field when we arrived and she began the practice herself, sending us on a three-mile run just like we had done in the preseason. She said she wanted to find out if our times had improved. I sure hoped we had improved 'cause Coach would make practices even tougher if we didn't.

I watched Brit, our manager, write down our scores on a clipboard and noticed that most of us had improved our times. Thank goodness! I looked up when someone said, "Here they come."

It was Coach and Tori with Jules following close behind. At least Tori **was** there. Maybe that was a good sign. I tried to read their faces, but couldn't tell from their expressions if things were going to be good or not. Coach called us into a huddle and took the clipboard from Brit.

Coach scanned the results of our run and beamed. "Very good. Your hard work has paid off." Then she turned to Tori and said, "Tori has something to say to the team."

I crossed my fingers behind my back. *Please let everything be all right.* I glanced at Sam next to me. She had her eyes closed, and seemed to be mouthing a little prayer.

"I want to apologize to the team for not being at practice on Saturday. I was thinking about qui…tting." Despite the rumor mill I still heard a few gasps as Tori said this and my stomach churned for her when she stumbled over the word 'quitting.'

I watched as she took a deep breath and went on. "I had a long talk with my sister and my good friend, Jackie. They helped me put some things in perspective. I really do want to b a part of this team. So … I'm sorry."

Coach put her hand on Tori's shoulder. "We've talked about this, what's good for Tori and what's good for the team. Tori will be staying with us. However she'll be sitting out the next game. Are there any questions?"

No one said a word, but I was sure there were a lot of different thoughts going on, but mostly I think we just wanted the moment to be over. It could have been anyone of us standing there having to own up to something stupid we did.

After practice Tori and I walked back to the gym together in silence. A few minutes later we were joined by Jules who threw her arm around my shoulder and said, "Thanks for helping Tori, She told me later what you said."

I smiled up at her. Maybe everything was going to be okay again between us. Then a moment later Jules said, "See ya," and bounded after Kate.

(14)

I had two big tests the next day, which, to my mind, wasn't fair at all. How could teachers expect anyone to concentrate when a person was trying to win the last two conference games and then get ready for states? As I finished up the second exam and put the paper on my algebra teacher's desk, I had some doubts about how I did 'cause it was a hard one.

That afternoon it felt strange taking the field for the game without Tori, and I was surprised when Coach announced who was taking her place. It was Cassie Henry. Coach said to a few of us, "Just keep talking to her, and she'll be fine."

Tori was Cassie's greatest rooter, shouting out support whenever Cassie got a little lost. Even with Tori's help I thought Cassie would be a train wreck. How could a beginner make so much progress to earn a starting position on our team? In fact she did miss the first two passes that came her way, the ball rolling out of bounds giving possession to the other team. But Heather Whitcraft, her midfield back-up, kept talking to her, and then changed the angle of her passes to Cassie so all Cassie had to do was run onto the ball. Pretty soon Cassie was blazing down the field with the ball safely on her stick. She looked like someone shot out of a cannon. No one could catch her.

At halftime Coach put in another player for Cassie, a senior who hadn't played much, but I think Coach got a chance to see what Cassie could do, and it was pretty impressive.

That night I got a phone call from the manager at the movie theater. "Can you come in Saturday afternoon? We'll give you a training session with concessions and see how it goes," he said.

After the phone call ended I ran downstairs and told Mom the good news. "That's great. I'll drop you off on my way to the hairdresser's." When she said that I realized I hadn't given any thought as to how I'd get to the theater. Could I count on Mom to drive me all the time? I decided I better go sign up for a 'Behind The Wheel' class first thing the next day.

When I got back to my bedroom my cell was ringing. It was Tori. "Hey, you want to do something this weekend?" she said.

"What happened to hunk-of-the-month?" I teased, thinking of the boy in her chemistry class who had driven her home after practice.

"Oh him. He's such a loser. Turns out the big flirt has another girl at St. Benedict's."

"Better you found out now. Still … it's only October. You have plenty of time to snag another guy before Christmas and the winter dance."

She laughed, and then we were back in a conversation like old times. I only hoped that before long Jules was back in my life, too.

*   *   *

The next day a major roadblock was thrown my way for getting to the state championship. Mr. Hoffner, my algebra teacher, handed back our test results. I looked at my paper. He had given me a D! *How could I have done so badly? He must have stayed up all night happily circling all my mistakes with his big fat Magic Marker. Maybe I was too stupid to even go to college.*

After he went over the correct answers for the class he said he wanted to see me at the end of the period. Everyone turned and stared at my face that I was sure was a bright shade of red. I sunk down in my seat wishing the world would open up and swallow me whole.

"Ms. McKendry, This isn't like you," Mr. Hoffner said when I came up to his desk. I stood there not knowing what to say. "Do you need a tutor?" he asked.

He was being pretty nice, so of course, I started to get all teary and said I didn't know.

"Besides getting a good grade, a lot of these topics will be found on the SATs, so it's important that you understand them," he said, as he put his roll book in a drawer and started to fill out a late pass for me. "There's a group that meets after school and does chapter reviews. Maybe that's what you need to do to bring up your grade."

"I have hockey."

"Maybe you should miss hockey and focus on your school work," he said. Now he was starting to sound like my mom, like hockey shouldn't be the most important thing in my life.

I'll think about it," I said. I began to take the late pass and that's when he said I better think about it if I wanted to go to college. I hurried down the hallway already late for gym. I was really starting to hate all this college stuff –

SAT's, vocab words, writing to schools. The pressure was building inside my head. I was ready to explode. *I JUST WANT TO PLAY HOCKEY!*

In the locker room I nearly collided with Coach as I raced around a corner to my aisle. "Good job yester ..." she started to say and then stopped when she saw how upset I was. What's the matter?"

A year ago I would have said, 'Nothing,' but I knew Coach better now. "I need to talk with you," I said.

"Okay," she said, and checked her watch. "I have a meeting right now and I'm running late. Stop in my office after class and I'll give you a note to get out of study hall." As I changed I felt a little better, like maybe Coach could bail me out of my algebra problems or tell colleges I was such a good player that they shouldn't worry about stupid SATs that I hadn't even taken yet.

Later when I explained what Mr. Hoffner wanted me to do I expected Coach was going to flip out. Instead she sat back in her chair. "Do you always struggle in math?"

"Not really. I mean I'm no brain, but I usually manage a B.

At this point of the season I think you can miss a half hour or so of practice 'til you get caught up. Why don't you find him before he goes home today. You can check with the captains on anything you miss."

Yeah, I thought, *I'll be sure to do that.* But at least she wasn't mad at me, so after school I hurried to Mr. Hoffner's room saying I was going to stay after school for help starting Friday.

"You made a good decision," Ms. McKendry. "I'm sure after a few afternoons you'll get back on track."

I hated the idea of missing a single second of hockey, but Coach seemed to think it was important so how could I argue. I thought the best plan would have been to have no more major tests on game days, but I guessed no one was going to listen to that idea.

After arranging for my 'algebra for dummies sessions,' I hurried to change and raced out to the field. I noticed we were at full strength. Tori was back and Coach was working on transition onto defense for us attackers, while Ms. Gillespie was working on defensive corners at the other end of the field, and Tori was with them. What was up with that I wondered?

I couldn't wonder for long though, as Coach had thrown us forwards in a 3v2 to goal drill. The big challenge of the drill was as soon as the attack scored or the ball went out-of-bounds Coach would throw out another ball to one of the defenders and we had to pressure these opposing players and double team the person with the ball or at least force her to the sideline.

Everyone was complaining under their breath how hard it was going from attack to defense so quickly. We hated doing it. But as we continued with the drill we saw how easy it was to score if we got the ball back and scoring goals always made attackers happy.

When we scrimmaged later I could see what Coach was up to with Tori. She had moved her back to her old midfield position, and had put Cassie up on varsity as the third forward with Sam and me. It was a risky move at this point in the season when we were getting ready to go after the conference title, but if it worked it could be awesome since we had not really found a third midfielder no matter who Coach had tried in that position. I couldn't wait for the next day's game to see what would happen.

Coach is brilliant. That's what ran through my mind in the closing minutes of our final regular season conference game. We were winning 6-0 and Cassie had just scored her first varsity goal ever. When I ran over and slapped her on the back to congratulate her she yelled in my ear, "This would never have happened if it wasn't for you."

My heart just about exploded out of my chest when she said that, and as I ran back to the center line for the restarting of play I wondered how many moments Coach had had like that over the years.

*   *   *

On Saturday, Mom dropped me off at the movie theater and as I got out of the car I looked up to the theater's marquee to see what was playing. There was a vampire movie, some French film I'd never watch, and two romantic comedies. It was a good mix and I wondered briefly if free movie passes were part of the deal when you worked there.

I took a deep breath and went inside to find the manager. Before I knocked on his door I quickly added a touch more lipstick to show I was a sophisticated grownup ready to work and not some kid trying to get in for half price. The guy came out and gave me a uniform shirt that I could wear over my clothes at the concession counter. "If things work out I can get you a different size," he said when he saw I kind of swam in the thing. He took me over to the girl working behind the concession counter, introduced us, and then he disappeared.

The girl's name was Carla Ramirez, a senior from St. Benedict's who had been working at the movie theater for about a year. We went through the 'who do you know' routine and it turned out there were quite a few people we knew in common, including of course, Chris Hanson. Her eyes sparkled when I mentioned his name. "He's so hot. The girls at school were all over him," she said. "But he never got serious with any of them. It made us wonder if he had a girlfriend at another school he wasn't talking about. I heard he went to prom, but nobody knew the girl." I decided maybe it was best not to mention I was that girl.

Finally we moved on to what my job was going to be. It was harder than it looked. Either people wanted their food really fast 'cause they were late for their show or they couldn't make up their minds what they wanted which made the people standing in line behind them want to kill them. The worst part though, was working the cash register. I could never remember in what order to push the buttons and then the darn thing wouldn't open. I was going to have to find Lizzie's old play register that was somewhere down in the basement and practice.

I only worked four hours, but it seemed like four days. I walked gloomily out of the theater waiting for Mom to pick me up sure I was going to be fired from a job before I officially even had it.

I called Tori when I got home begging off the movie date we had arranged. I told her I was so exhausted from working I needed to sleep. She laughed, "Stood up by Mr. Big Flirt and now you. If I didn't know any better I'd say I was a social pariah."

I had to think a minute what a pariah was, sure it was not on the SAT word list, and then finally figured it out. It made me wonder how I was ever going to take the SATs. After we had said goodbye I realized what was good about Tori was that she never got hung up about the small stuff. A lot of girls would have been all up in your face telling you that you had ruined their lives simply because you were too tired to go out.

* * *

The following Tuesday was our conference championship game. Northfield represented the North Division of our league and Henderson represented the South. A coin toss determined the home field site. They won, so we were traveling there. When I opened my locker during eighth period for our early dismissal from school I found another note. It simply said —

Good luck

I looked around the hallway which was kind of stupid since I was the only one there. But I did have a little hope that the writer would show themselves, maybe like jumping out of a doorway and shouting "surprise." Why couldn't they simply sign it? Why had they typed it? I slammed the locker door in frustration. I really wanted to know who was leaving these notes.

We could see a scattering of blue and white balloons for Northfield and red and black ones in Henderson's colors as soon as our bus pulled up next to the field. I was surprised by how many fans were already there from both schools.

Just before we were to start the game I noticed Noah waving his arms wildly about as he tried to get our attention. He must have driven over as soon as school let out. With him were his ever-present girlfriend, James, and Will. I nudged Anna to let her know her own personal fan club had arrived. She glanced over, but didn't dare wave since Coach was in the middle of one of her intense pre-game strategy talks and wouldn't have appreciated someone not attending to her every word.

For much of the game the ball went back and forth, like two fighters trading punches until one makes a mistake leaving an opening for their opponent to land the final blow. It was the kind of game I enjoyed and it was just what we needed to get ready for the start of the state tournament the following week.

We got them early in the second half when Tori sent me a sweet pass down the line. I beat one defender and there was just the goalkeeper left. She started to go out on me, then hesitated. It was all I needed as I saw Sam catching up with me, and at the last moment I slipped her the ball for an easy score. As I jogged back to the center I remember Coach always telling our defenders, "Once you make up your mind, don't hesitate." She sure got that right.

That was our only score of the game, but it was enough. As we raised the league plaque above our heads I smiled knowing it would be sitting in our school's trophy case for at least a year and wondered if there was going to be room in the case for a trophy or two as well.

Our team's parents had a field day taking pictures. Both my mom and dad made the game which was very cool, and we all laughed in amusement watching Lizzie as she angled to get her picture taken with her beloved Tori. I was just a little sad that Mr. Hanson couldn't be there to see this happy event, but it was his own fault for sure.

*   *   *

The next day Coach was supposed to hear about the pairings for the state tournament. I was dragging my feet getting changed for gym, hoping for some news from Coach, when Anna and Sam came over to me and asked if I knew anything yet. When I shook my head, Sam said, "Let's go check in Coach's office. Maybe she's got the word by now." Normally I would never go near the coaches' offices 'cause I didn't want to be a bother when they were probably busy, and wouldn't know what to say to them anyway, but this time it seemed legit.

Sam knocked on the closed door and when it opened Jules was standing there. That was when I saw Kate sitting in a chair talking to Coach and Ms. O'Donnell who was just grabbing her roll-book off her desk.

"We better get to class," I said, backing out the door feeling foolish like we had interrupted some big powwow or something.

Ms. O'Donnell looked over her shoulder at Coach, "Sam can stay. She can let Anna and Jackie know later."

Anna and I followed Ms. O'Donnell out to the gym where she took roll and we all grabbed some old lacrosse sticks and headed out to the field.

"Secret meeting?" Anna asked as she walked along side me.

"There are no secret meetings," Ms. O'Donnell said from behind us. Anna and I looked at each other wondering how much she had overheard. Lucky for us, she was smiling.

"You girls have the funniest ideas," she said. "Mrs. Fortunata always has captains meetings once a week if players class schedules allow it.

Okay, I thought, *maybe not so awkward that we were at the door then.* I heard footsteps pounding behind us and then Sam pounced on my back. "Hey, we have a first-round bye. We're going to play the winner of the Browns-Mills/New Elizabeth game next Tuesday.

Anna and I looked at each other feeling the excitement of Sam's announcement build up in us. Then Sam added, "And we're ranked number two in Group Four."

We all high fived each other and danced around a bit feeling the rush of the news now that we learned how high we were ranked in South Jersey, at least among the schools with the biggest school populations.

"Who's number one?" Ms. O'Donnell asked. I could feel her adrenaline pumping, too, and why not? After all we were her babies, the first players she had coached.

"Some school down near the shore. I forget their name," Sam said.

So we were set. The road map to the state championship was revealed to us. All we had to do was stay on course.

(15)

At practice, during a water break, Lindsay came up to me. "How about all the trash talk on the hockey forum?" she said.

"What are you talking about?"

"What do you mean what am I talking about? You're on it, too. I see what you write."

I tossed the rest of the water away, and threw the paper cup in the trashcan while I tried to make sense of what Lindsay was saying. Finally I turned back to her. "Linds, I'm not on any forum."

"Aren't you jacmcshootr? That's what you use for your email address."

"Yes, but … Lindsay, it's not me on the forum."

"Then someone knows your email and is using it to pretend to be you. I mean, you never write your real name or anything …"I frowned. She went on, "Still, whoever it is they're writing like they're you, and what they say is definitely pro Northfield, and not very nice for the other schools. Personally, I think it's great."

That night I had to study for a big Spanish test and didn't have time to check out the hockey forum. I didn't think of it again 'til I got to lunch and told Anna and Sam what Lindsay had said, but they weren't much help.

Will looked up from his paperback. "Maybe you can keep tabs on it for a while, and if your real name is used you can contact the webmaster and he can put a block on the person," he said.

"Never mind all that. Don't forget about tomorrow," Noah said. All of a sudden the hockey forum was forgotten as there was a rush to figure out how we were going to get into the city to see the band at the Longstreet Pier. We decided to meet up at the Patco Speedline, the train that would take us across the river, and then walk the few blocks to the pier. Everyone at the table was going, even Sam. I was psyched that she was able to get away from her responsibilities at home and have some fun for a change.

That night the theater manager called and told me I had gotten the job, and to come in on Sunday and they would go through my work schedule. After he hung up, I whooped in the air and then looked around my room. It's hard to explain, but it didn't seem like a kid's room anymore. I had a real job. All of a sudden I felt very grown up.

Unfortunately my phone call from the theater manager wasn't the only phone call at the McKendry house that night. Sometime in the night I woke to the ringing of the house phone. I heard some voices and then must have fallen back to sleep. Mom woke me to tell me my Grandma McKendry had been rushed to the hospital. She and Dad were about to leave for the shore and I had to watch Lizzie the next day until they could get home.

"What about practice?" I said to my mom as she turned to leave.

"Either take her with you or stay home. I've got to go," she said. As she hurried from the room she looked over her shoulder. "Jackie, I'm counting on you."

I lay there in the dark with a ton of thoughts running through my head. My grandma was always such an energetic person. I couldn't imagine her sick. And my dad had to be so worried driving in the middle of the night to find out what was going on with his mom. I couldn't bear it if anything happened to my parents no matter how old they got.

I looked at the bedroom clock — *four-thirty*. I got up and tried to do some reading, but it was no use. Too much was running through my mind. Finally I powered up my computer and found myself gravitating toward the hockey forum. Some of it was just a bunch of parents sounding off about how their kids were better than some other school's kids, or bashing some club coach for not making their kids into the superstars the parents were sure they were meant to be. *Get a life, peeps,* I thought.

But the really vicious messages were from kids like myself, trashing certain teams. I knew they were from kids 'cause of how they wrote not caring about spelling and punctuation. The adults always had their commas in the right places. I looked for any more messages from my 'alter-ego' and was relieved to find none. *Maybe they got tired of writing, or maybe their season was over and they didn't care anymore.*

I checked the clock again. *Just past five.* I went to my email figuring I might as well do something productive. There were three more messages from college coaches. Two were from schools so far away that I thought I'd need a passport to enroll, so I sent them a 'thanks, but no thanks.' The third was from Coach's' friend. I decided since the school wasn't too far away I'd write her back saying I'd like more information, and promised to fill out the recruiting form on her web site. *Dad would be proud*

I thought about signing off and then I remembered the YouTube video. I hadn't wanted to look at it before 'cause hearing the words made me too sad even if it was over a year ago when I wrote them. But now that Mitch was back, and wasn't interested in being my boyfriend anymore, maybe I needed to face it and put the past behind me. I scrolled to the tag for the video and pressed play. The band looked good and the song actually sounded better than the first time I had heard the guys play it. I was so taken in by the camerawork that I could almost accept the video as some stranger's song, and then the band got to the chorus and I was done in by the harmonizing of James and Noah and quickly pressed pause. Jeez ... over thirty thousand hits. There wouldn't be another one coming from me. *Sorry Boys.* I was exhausted.

Finally the sun rose and I showered even though I would be all sweaty in a few hours. I needed to wake up. At seventy-thirty I tried dragging Lizzie out of bed and she was having none of it. "Where's Mom?" she wailed.

I explained about Grandma, but wasn't getting anywhere as Lizzie pulled the covers up around her. "Look, I don't care if you want to sleep," I said. "I'd like to get some sleep, too, but I've got to get to practice. Now move it." I went to her closet and pulled out some jeans and a long sleeved tee-shirt and threw them on the bed. "Hurry up and get dressed."

"I'm not wearing that," she said, as she sat up and crossed her arms over her chest in a fit of mutiny at my selections.

Then I played my last card before I resorted to physical force. "Tori loves you in blue. She told me. But if you don't want to see her then just forget it." It worked. All of a sudden my sister exploded into action rushing to the bathroom to brush her teeth. I hurried downstairs. I had just enough time to get out some milk and cereal for Lizzie with some time left over to make her a snack. Fifteen minutes later we were sitting on the front step waiting for Mrs. Hanson.

The twins looked surprised when Lizzie hopped in the back seat next to Tori. When I explained about my grandma Mrs. Hanson said she'd be glad to pick us up after practice and to call her if I needed anything else.

Tori picked up on the situation snuggling into Lizzie and saying, "I missed you so much. When are we going to have that sleepover together?" My sister finally smiled. And the two princesses were off in a marathon discussion of modeling and girly fashions. I sent Tori a silent thanks and slumped down in the seat feeling exhausted, and wondered how I was going to get through the next two hours of practice.

When we got to the field I put Lizzie on the bench with her snack, telling her if she wanted some water she could ask our managers. She eyed Brit and Nadja as potential 'Lizzie fans' and brightened.

As I walked over to Coach she gave me a troubled look as she had already spotted Lizzie deep in conversation with our managers. "What's up, Jackie?" she asked.

"Coach, I'm so sorry. I know Lizzie shouldn't be here," and then I explained about the phone call in the night and how my mom told me I had to have Lizzie with me or miss practice.

"You know our policy about not having distractions." I nodded. Coach had sent home team rules to all the parents in the beginning of the season, and guessed that using practice for babysitting was not on the agenda for a good working environment for athletes. She patted my shoulder. "I realize it must have been an emergency. Just this once, right?" she said. I nodded and raced off to put on my cleats.

For once I was relieved when practice was over. All I wanted to do was sleep. Driving home in the car Tori reminded me about the concert at the Longstreet Pier. I had completely forgotten about it.

"What time are you guys leaving for the train?" I asked, looking at Lizzie and wondering if my parents would be back in time to take her off my hands.

"Around one. Don't worry. We can pick you up," Tori said.

And that's how we left it. When we got home I raced upstairs to shower and left Lizzie playing in the family room. Twenty-five minutes later I was downstairs and found Lizzie on the computer that Mom kept on a small desk in the kitchen. "What are you doing?" I said.

She quickly clicked the power off and then turned to face me. She shrugged and said, "Nothing."

I had no time to cross-examine her as the Hansons would be picking me up in a half hour. I popped some frozen pizzas in the toaster oven and started going through my bag to be sure I had enough money for the trip into Philly. I checked my watch. *Where were Mom and Dad?* Then it hit me. Suppose something really bad had happened to Grandma? I tried Mom's cell phone, but didn't get any response. What was going on?

At one o'clock Jules rang the door bell. When I answered, I shook my head. "Can't make it. They're not back yet."

"Do you want my mom to watch Lizzie? It'd be a shame for you to miss it."

It sounded tempting, but I remembered Mom saying she was counting on me and that probably didn't mean somebody else. "I better stay with Lizzie," I said, and told Jules to go on and have a good time.

I got a phone call an hour later. It was my mom. "Sorry I couldn't get a hold of you sooner. There is no reception on the hospital's emergency floor and we didn't want to leave Grandma."

"What happened? Is she going to be okay?"

"I'm getting in the car now and I'll tell you everything when I get home. Dad is staying here with Grandma. Is Lizzie okay?"

I was relieved it was me that could say she was, and wondered how frantic Mom would have been if she couldn't track me down and wondered what happened to Lizzie. Once I was off the phone I looked at the afternoon ahead. Lizzie was busy watching something on the Disney Channel so I figured I might as well get some schoolwork done and went upstairs.

A little over an hour later my mom walked in the door. From her weary face I could tell the news was not good. She plopped down on the overstuffed couch in the family room, dropped her pocketbook and car keys to the floor, then closed her eyes. Any sulkiness I felt over missing the Battle of the Bands quickly disappeared.

Lizzie, who had been lying on the floor in front of the TV, finally looked up from the show she was watching. "Mommy," she squealed, running over and hugging my mom.

"Leave Mom alone. Can't you see she's tired?" I said crossly.

"It's okay, Jackie," Mom said, and wrapped her arms around my sister. Then she turned to me. "I'm glad I could count on you." She gave me a long look and then smiled. "You look as bad as I do. Kind of a sleepless night all around I guess."

Before I could answer, Lizzie said, "She was supposed to go to a concert with the twins and Mrs. Hanson said she'd watch me."

"Sorry, Jackie," Mom said, and then she turned to my sister. "It's a nice day out. Why don't you go play out back? I want to talk to Jackie."

Lizzie reluctantly grabbed her jacket and went outside and my mom patted the seat next to her for me to sit. "Grandma was at her bridge club last night and started getting chest pains. Fortunately she said something to her friends and they drove her right to the hospital. She's had a heart attack."

I felt my blood turn cold and could hardly breathe. "But Grandma isn't that old, I finally said. "She's always running around. She does Yoga twice a week." I couldn't get my head around it.

My mom took me in her arms. "I know. I know." Then she pulled away. "Being so active is probably what's keeping her alive right now."

I slumped back in the couch. "What's going to happen?"

My mom leaned back on the couch, too, and stared out the window at my sister who was playing on the old swing in the backyard. Then she took my hand still watching my sister. "We don't know Jackie. We just don't know."

Mom finally roused herself and said, "Let's order some Chinese for dinner. Then we'll wait to hear from Dad if he has any news.

I started to get the phone and then remembered. "Mom, I'm supposed to work tomorrow. What should I do?"

She put her arm around me. "We'll work things out. Don't worry."

(16)

My dad stayed at the hospital that night. By the next morning there had been little change in Grandma's condition. My parents decided that Matt would come home from college and take Mom to the hospital to be with my dad, and after Matt saw Grandma, he'd come home.

"I've already made arrangements with the Hansons to take Lizzie for the day," Mom said, as she poured herself a cup of coffee. "They'll take you to your job, too, and then Matt will pick you up when you're done work."

"But I want to see Grandma, too."

"Only one person at a time is allowed in intensive care. She's sleeping and I think we should wait a bit. Don't worry. We'll make sure you have a chance to see her."

When my brother arrived, he and Mom left for the hospital almost immediately, and I was left alone with Lizzie. I felt like a little girl again – old enough maybe to watch my sister, but not old enough to handle my grandma being so sick. I wandered restlessly around the house until it was time to dress for work.

When Mrs. Hanson picked us up, both Jules and Tori were with her. "We're sorry about your Grandma," Jules said, giving me a hug. "We've always had so much fun every time you took us to her shore house."

"Yeah, she's the best," Tori said, as she pulled Lizzie into the car with her.

"How was the concert?" I asked, following Lizzie into the backseat.

"Awesome," Tori said excitedly. Then she seemed to remember why I couldn't be there, and said more quietly, "Maybe you could call when you get home from work and we can fill you in."

My job at the theater was a lot easier this time. I wasn't working concessions with Carla, but a girl who was a senior from my own school. She helped me with the cash register 'til I finally got it. When the lines for popcorn and sodas dwindled away, she started cracking jokes, and giving me the lowdown on some of the other seniors at our school which really helped me forget my family stuff for a while. At the end of my shift the manager came out and we discussed when I could work. I explained about my hockey season being over in a couple of weeks which would increase the time he'd expect me to work.

Matt was waiting for me when I came out of the theater. It felt so good to be back in his old car again. It reminded me of all the times he had taken me to school freshman year. I remember one day I had persuaded him to drive me to the town library where I could meet up with Mitch. Matt had given Mitch the 'I'm the big brother you better be nice to my sister talk.' I could laugh about it now, but I was mortified at the time.

"How's Grandma? Did you see her?" I asked, as he made the turn onto the road for the Hansons.

"I'm not gonna lie, Jack, she's not good," he said. "I think I overheard them saying the next forty-eight hours are critical. They put in two stents to open up her arteries. They're hoping that's all they have to do."

The tears started rolling down my face. I reached into my pockets to find a tissue, but came up empty. "Box on the floor," Matt said. He looked at my face. "We have to stay strong for Mom and Dad. Okay?" I nodded.

We pulled into the Hanson's long driveway and my brother went to the door to get Lizzie, giving me enough time to get myself together.

Lizzie was bouncing in the backseat all the way home telling stories about how much fun she had with Tori and Jules. "We watched movies, and then I did some drawings with Tori. She said I was really good." I listened to my sister babble on glad that someone in the McKendry family had a good day.

I phoned the twins after we settled Lizzie. "Thanks for watching Lizzie," I said to Tori. "You guys are great." I told her a bit about my grandma, and then asked about the concert. She gave me the main points explaining that the band hadn't won, but should have, and then she said something that totally startled me. "Mitch was there."

"What? You're kidding!" *Was he with someone* I wanted to ask, but was afraid to know the truth.

"Yeah, anyhow I don't think he stayed the whole time. I know he saw the band, and then he kind of disappeared. He wasn't standing with us anyhow."

After the news of Mitch being at the concert my emotions were bouncing all over the place. I was tired and up to my eyeballs with the pressures of the day. After we ended the call I went downstairs to say goodbye to Matt, who was heading back to school as soon as Mom and Dad came home. Then I crawled in bed, wishing I could sleep for a hundred days.

*   *   *

Both my mom and dad were sitting at the kitchen table when I came down the next morning. My dad looked like he had aged a ton in the last few days. I mean, I got it, too. Grandma was his mom. I glanced at my mom, who was watching my dad with such a loving expression on her face. What would it be like if anything happened to her?

When he heard me come in, Dad reached out and gave me a hug. "Thanks for your help yesterday, Jackie. Grandma is a tough cookie. She's going to pull through this. You'll see."

"I'm really sorry Dad. I hope I can see Grandma soon."

"Me, too. Get some breakfast, then I'll drop you off at school on my way back down the shore.

I brightened. No school bus — a good way to start the week. After my Dad dropped me off, and I made my way to my locker, I felt relieved to be walking down the familiar hallway, like it was some kind of normal day. I needed to put my family stuff in my back pocket for a while, even if only for a few hours.

At lunch there was some rehashing of the Battle of the Bands. Anna said she thought Noah and James's band should have won, and Will agreed. "You guys were robbed," he said. "You sounded great and James's singing is awesome."Noah frowned a little. It made me wonder if there was some jealousy between him and James, and if so how long the band could really stay together if there really was a problem.

I asked James about it in English class. "We're working on making it work," he said, as he doodled in the margins of his notebook. He tossed down his pencil. "Truthfully, I give us another year, which is a pretty long time for a band like ours to stay together. I'm planning on college or a music school, and so is Eric, our drummer. Noah isn't interested in anything like that. He wants to travel and get his career going."

His comments made me think of my friendship with Jules and Tori. Were we destined to all go in different directions? Did we only have a year left, too?

After algebra help I discovered the team had just started a thirty minute run. "You can catch up with them," Coach said. Even though I wasn't starting out with the others, a run was just what I needed. Although some players hated the runs, for me it was a time to relax and feel free. I caught up with Anna as she was entering the neighboring development. "How's your grandmother?" she asked. "Jules told me about her at the Battle of the Bands."

I shrugged my shoulders and was noncommittal.

Anna must have sensed I didn't want to talk about it 'cause she changed the subject. "Anyway," she said, "We missed you. I went with Will." I nodded since I already knew the whole table was going. "No, I mean I went with Will."

My eyes widened and gave her a fist bump. She danced around in a little circle. "Yeah," she said, resuming her pace, "He actually asked me to go with him. His dad drove us to the train station where we met the others. And ..." Her eyes were gleaming now. "He asked me out for next Saturday night."

"Good for you," I said.

Her face got more serious, and she seemed to be studying me. "We met up with your old boyfriend, Mitch Kennedy. He's a nice guy. I can see why Will likes him so much. Can I ask what ever happened with you guys?"

My throat started to close up and it became harder to breath. We passed a couple more houses. Then I said, "You know he left school last year, right?" She nodded. "He told me the night he left not to think he'd be back." I thought about how much I could trust Anna and then I said, "I've told nobody. Nobody, okay?" She looked up surprised, and I went on. "You know the video the band recorded? The song? It's mine. I mean the words are mostly, with a little help from James. I wrote it when Mitch left."

I could see her thinking about the lyrics, and then she turned to me and there were tears in her eyes. "I get it. I really do," she said quietly.

I gave her a small smile, then decided to move on to a safer topic. "So, how badly are we going to beat Sea Isle Township?"

"Badly, very, very badly," she said, as we rounded the bend and had the school in our sights, and then she picked up the pace, racing me the last 200 yards to the field.

When I got home that night there was no more news about Grandma, so I guessed that was a good thing. Mom even said they would take me to see her soon. After dinner was over I was wandering the house aimlessly as it was one of the few nights without much homework. I noticed the basement door open and a light on at the bottom of the stairs. Curious I jogged down the steps and found my dad in the storage section, rooting through a bunch of plastic containers.

"Whatcha doing?" I asked, peering over his shoulder.

"Needed some mental R&R. It's almost Halloween and we haven't done anything. I thought I'd better get some decorations out before the kids come trick or treating."

"Here, let me help," I said, and so for the next half hour we sorted through our stash of cats, monsters, and pumpkins. We tossed out a few broken pieces and had a laugh or two about old memories of past Halloweens when we came across the scary witch that made me almost wet my pants when I was little, and a string of ghost lights that were favorites of mine we had gotten just a couple of years ago that were the hit of our block. We brought everything upstairs and showed the decorations to Mom. It looked like she needed a mental boost, too, as she immediately started putting some fake pumpkins around the living room fireplace.

It seemed to have lightened my dad's mood and for that I was glad. I decided to go upstairs and do some sorting of my own, going to my closet and pulling out the file folder that Dad had bought me. Then I scattered the packets and letters across my bed deciding where to begin. *Who should I tackle first? Should it be alphabetical like the file folder, by distance from home, or by the order in which they were postmarked?* Finally I decided on postmarks, figuring that was fairest. I sorted them and then pulled the first three off the top.

The first was from the school in Virginia where we attended the hockey camp. I remembered one of my coaches there telling our team that she was an assistant coach at the school. *How could she have remembered me? Probably it was my red hair, and besides that my pale skin made me the only girl at camp without a fabulous summer tan.*

The second was from a school out west that I had never heard of. Too far I decided, and made it my first personal reject. The third was from the school where my parents went to college. It was in Iowa. I logged onto my computer, since I kind of forgot where Iowa was, and discovered that it wasn't exactly at the end of the world. It made the school a possible 'keeper.'

I grabbed the packets of the two 'possibles,' and headed downstairs to find my dad. "I wondered when you'd be ready to do this," he said, eyeing the packets. I handed him the two envelopes and he grinned. "So you could be a legacy," he said. He saw my puzzled look and explained that was what the son or daughter of an alum was called.

"Should I go there then?"

"No, no. You need to think about a lot of things before you decide on a school. But it's a good place to start. Then he explained what I should write in a letter or in most cases in an email.

Sitting down at my desk, knowing what to write, and remembering I had to hit SpellCheck so coaches didn't cross out my name thinking I was too stupid to go to their school, made me feel like I was going about things the right way.

I tackled my reject school first with an email telling them thank you very much, but wasn't interested. Always best to be honest and polite was what Dad had told me.

The second packet, from the Virginia school, took more time. At least I knew about that school and had walked around their campus which seemed kind of big to me. On the plus side, their assistant coach was pretty nice so I decided to email them saying I liked their school and was filling out their online recruiting form. I also let them know we were playing in the state tournament and we had won the conference title. Dad also said you were supposed to tell them what was happening with your season. I guessed they didn't want to hear about an old boyfriend back at school or a sick Grandma, so I decided to end it there and pushed send.

I looked through the information my parents' school had sent me. I wondered if their coach had been at the invitational camp Jules and I had attended 'cause I didn't know how she would know anything about me otherwise. I thumbed through their hockey brochure. They had a player from California and another from Canada. I thought it sure took guts to go to school in another country even if you did speak the same language. Maybe the program was really good. I looked them up online. Yep, they were doing well this year, too. So they became the second carefully worded email sent. I told the coach my dad had played soccer there about a 'million' years ago figuring that might help, too.

I surveyed the results of my work. It felt good to put one packet in a reject pile, like I was starting to make some decisions. It wasn't as bad as I thought. *Maybe I could really do this college thing.*

(17)

The day of our first state tournament game started out sunny and bright, but by sixth period lunch, the clouds were rolling in. Noah checked the weather report on his phone. "It says occasional showers in the afternoon."

"That's not bad," Sam said. "As long as there's no lightning we should get the game in." And she was right. Except for one low area, which we had learned to avoid a long time ago after some major slides on our butts, our field had good drainage. So things were looking pretty good for the game.

As I was making my way to my last class of the day, I thought how stupid it was to go at all. I only had ten minutes before I'd be dismissed for the game. My darker side figured it was the job of schools to make you as miserable as long as they possibly could.

"You look pretty happy. What's up?" James asked as he eyed my uniform shirt when I slid into the seat next to him.

"Same old, same old," I said, pretending to stifle a yawn.

"Maybe you need some excitement in your life. Maybe," he paused dramatically and pretended to stroke a mustache like an old-time villain, "Maybe what you need is a new man."

"I'll get on that," I said, glancing up at the clock, "But not right now. Gotta get to the game."

Racing down the empty corridor to my hall locker, I quickly dialed my combination and that's when I opened my locker to find another note wishing me well in my game. *Maybe this could be my 'new man'* I thought, a secret admirer like in the movies. I laughed at my silliness as I hurried back down the hallway to the locker room. *It probably wasn't even a guy, probably it was someone on the team. Maybe Cassie or her sister. Yeah, it could be either of them.*

I'd like to say something memorable about the game, but there was nothing, not even a little rain. The other team, whose record was barely five hundred, never had a chance. I scored four easy goals and was taken out in the last ten minutes with the score 6-0. The big thing was what happened afterward. Some reporter guy stuck a microphone in front of my face and asked a bunch of stupid questions. "How does it feel to be the leading scorer?" "Who do you want to face next?" How can a person answer stuff like that?

I told him my teammates made it easy for me to score 'cause their passes were always so great. I didn't know what to say to the other question. I didn't even know who else was playing that day. Coach saved me by coming up and saying we were really looking forward to our next game whoever it was.

She walked away with me and whispered, "I'll give you some lessons on handling reporters tomorrow.

"How about I never have to speak to one again?" I said hopefully.

She patted my shoulder. "I don't think that's going to happen." Then as she walked away she said. "Good game, Jackie."

My dad was at the game and afterward he said, "I brought another shirt if you need it. We're going to the shore. It's time you saw your grandmother."

It turned into one of those great rides you sometimes have with a parent. You have them all to yourself with no competition from a brother or sister. Best of all you're not being lectured about something you did wrong, like "you should be doing better in math" or "your room is a mess," or something. We stopped halfway for some juicy burgers and wolfed them down, both of us making a sloppy mess, and not caring at all.

I slipped on the shirt Dad had brought me and pulled on my sweats before we went into the hospital. Walking to my Grandma's room Dad warned we couldn't stay too long. He touched my arm before I went in. "Don't be upset when you see the tubes and IVs. She **is** doing a little better."

I was glad Dad prepared me. Grandma looked so little and frail lying on the bed. She seemed to be asleep. The only sound in the room was the steady beep of a machine that looked like it was monitoring her heart. I moved closer to the bed. Grandma must have sensed me there 'cause her eyes fluttered open.

"Jackie," she said in a weak voice.

"Don't try to talk," I said, trying to find a spot on her arm I could touch without disturbing all the tubes that seemed to be everywhere.

"Don't you worry, I'm stronger than I look," she said with difficulty through her cracked lips. "My mouth is dry. Get me a little water." She motioned toward the stand by her bed. I looked around and saw the straw sticking out of a Styrofoam cup. After she took a few sips her voice sounded a little better. "It's all going to be okay. They're going to fix me up and I'll be running around before you know it."

"I love you Grandma," I said.

"I love you, too, honey." She saw the tears in my eyes. "Now listen, you and I are made of good Scottish stock. We can weather anything and don't you forget it. Okay?" I nodded, afraid to speak 'cause my voice might break. "You scored today, right?" And for the first time I smiled.

"Good, now go get your father. I want to speak to him."

I kissed her forehead and went to find my dad. He was in with Grandma only a short time.

"Thanks for taking me," I said, grabbing his hand as we walked through the mostly deserted parking lot. He gave my hand a squeeze and I knew he was glad I'd been with him. Our ride home was pretty quiet. It had been such a long day I must have dozed off and didn't wake until we reached our development.

Dad tugged at my ponytail. "Good nap?" he said.

I nodded. "I'm glad I saw Grandma. Is she really going to be okay?"

"I think so. Your grandma's a survivor. You know, she raised me on her own and got us through some rough times."

I felt I was on the verge of a family history lesson and wanted to know more. "When did Grandpop McKendry die? What happened?"

He died in a fire. Fell through a burning staircase and landed two floors below. I was seven at the time."

"So he was a fireman, right?"

"Yep, big city in North Jersey. After the insurance claims and pension were settled, your grandma wanted to move out of the city and find some quiet place to live. It was right before casinos, the shore area not so built up as it is now. Grandma found a nice property along the bay. A double lot with an old fishing shack going for cheap. She went back to school and got her teaching degree and then she went to work fixing up that old shack 'til it became what you see today.

I pictured the gray shingled cottage with its cozy back porch. The house was small, for sure, but was cute as could be. We had pulled into our driveway, but I wanted to hear more. "She did it all on her own?"

"Pretty much. If she couldn't do it herself she talked somebody else into helping her out or traded tutoring hours for construction hours." My dad turned off the motor and leaned back in his seat. "Better get to bed honey."

I reached over and gave my dad a kiss on the cheek. I wouldn't have traded that night with my dad for anything.

*   *   *

The next day when I came down for breakfast I found my dad trying to read the paper, only it wasn't his usual 'go to' section — sports. I peered over his shoulder at the fashion page. "What's up Dad? You losing it?"

Your mother grabbed the paper before I could even get at it," he said, grinning up at me.

"The twin's mom texted me this morning and put me on alert," Mom said, as she put the carefully folded-up paper on the table. It was the high school sports page. Right in the upper left hand corner, already circled in red Magic Marker, was an action shot of me with the ball, being chased by some girl from the other team. Beneath the words, *Northfield's McKendry Outruns Sea Isle.* I picked up the paper and quickly scanned the article beneath the picture relieved to discover none of my quotes had been used, since nothing I said had made any sense. However, there was a quote by Jules. "Jackie McKendry is the heart of our team. She might have scored four goals today, but she is the most unselfish player I know."

"Wasn't that nice of Jules?" Mom said.

I swallowed hard, nodded, and put the paper down. I went to the frig to get myself some juice hoping it would give get rid of the lump in my throat. *I am such a jerk. I don't deserve your friendship, Jules.*

When I opened my locker I was kind of surprised not to see any paper falling out of my locker. *Maybe my mystery writer's printer ran out of ink*, I thought, a little disappointed. I had to admit that I had been getting a little jolt of pleasure every time a note had landed at my feet. A couple people did comment on my photo as I went through my morning, though.

At lunch Will teased me big-time about the newspaper article, tearing a piece of paper out of his notebook and asking for my autograph.

"Sorry," I said, pushing the paper back to him. "I only do signings at conventions." He laughed and went back to reading his latest paperback.

"Seriously," Anna said, "it was a great pic and the article was awesome. It's about time we got some press.

"Yeah, but we already did. Remember *New Gretna Delivers Fatal Blow?*" I said.

Anna scrunched up her face. Then the whole table got into a heated discussion between good press, bad press, versus no press at all. Noah said he loved reading great reviews of his band.

"But what if they say you stink?" Sam said.

Noah chuckled. "Only the hard-of-hearing would ever say that."

Noah sure seemed confident which was so different than James. I wondered if staying together for another year was being too optimistic on James' part.

Practice that day was jam-packed, Coach ticking off each thing we needed to cover for the day. Mainly it was all about keeping us in shape and fine-tuning just a couple of things that could make a difference in a close game. The time seemed to fly, and I wondered if it was like that with every successful season, if the players realized how fast the end was coming, and if they tried to hold onto every minute for all it were worth knowing they couldn't ever get that time back again.

That night I was deep into answering a set of questions on my latest novel for English when my cell rang. Not recognizing the area code, I meant to push the end button when the question sheet fell off my lap, and not paying attention, wound up pushing the wrong button.

"Hey, Jackie," I heard as I lifted the phone to my ear. "It's Chris."

"This isn't your cell," I said dumbly.

"No, I know. It's my roommate's. Mine's charging. My sisters' told me about your grandma. How are things going?"

"It's kind of scary. I never thought my grandma would get sick. I mean she's so healthy, or … at least she was."

"It made me think of my nana over in Italy. We're so far away. If anything happened …" his voiced trailed away.

The conversation was getting kind of sad, so I changed the subject. "Hey, I scored my first goal of the season for you."

He chuckled. "I was counting on that."

We talked for a few more minutes, and then he said he was sorry he couldn't see any of the upcoming games, but wished me luck.

As I resumed working on my English assignment I felt a little peppier. I didn't know what it was about the twins' brother, but every time he popped up in my life my thoughts turned a little sunnier. I figured it must be a gift he had and someday he would make the girl in his life a very lucky person.

Before I went to bed I decided to check out the hockey forum. It had been a while and I wanted to make sure my alternate self wasn't talking more trash. I scrolled down the posts and picked out a comment that I was sure was from Lindsay. It said how the team was on top of their game and was ready to take on the world including our next opponent, Somerville High.

Then I looked further and gasped. There were two posts from jacmcshootr, and both were awful. Sommerville was getting slammed and the worst comment was, "Jackie McKendry is going to shoot up Sommerville's defense. Count on it." *What was I going to do?*

We talked about it at lunch the next day. "Somebody sure loves you," Anna joked.

"It's embarrassing," I wailed.

"You guys shouldn't pay attention to any of that stuff," Will said. "In basketball people are always talking trash. It's even worse on the court."

"Hey Jack, if they jump all over you, I'll be able to score all the goals we need," Sam said. "Don't worry about it."

But I did, and as it turned out, I was right to.

(18)

Friday was the third round of states. It would be our last time to play at home. If we won, all the rest of the games would be held at neutral sites at predetermined schools. I felt nervous all day. Not good butterfly nervous, on edge nervous. I really needed to forget about that stupid hockey forum!

The only good thing happening that day was that my mystery writer was back, wishing me luck. I patted my jeans pocket feeling the note, hoping it would calm me down. Only it didn't help. Did that mean we were going to lose today? Was our journey going to end as abruptly as last year? I felt a chill run up my back, and it had nothing to do with the coolness in the air on this early November day.

I was disappointed my parents weren't going to be at the game. They were moving Grandma to a cardiac rehabilitation center around noon and didn't think they'd make it back in time.

After the warm-up, our manager, Nadja, announced the starting players. She always brought a smile to our team 'cause her Indian accent sounded so 'upper crust,' her annunciation of each of our names making us seem more important than we really were. Each of us jogged over to shake the opposing coach's hand and then we lined up on the field for the national anthem.

As I joined my teammates on the field, I noticed a couple of the Somerville players whispering among themselves and glaring at me. I tried to block out the feelings of paranoia that were creeping up my back. I glanced at my teammates standing on either side of me who seemed to be bouncing out of their skins as the anthem was being sung by one of the members of our school's chorus. I shook my head trying to make the uneasiness I was feeling go away, hoping it was all just pre-game nerves.

Even though we dominated the game, almost from the opening minute, Somerville dug in and fought hard every time we approached their goal. I hadn't taken a single shot as the half ended, and twice was sent sprawling to the ground as I cut into the circle. The score was still 0-0 midway through the second half, and I could feel the tide turning in Somerville's favor as they started getting some fast breaks down the field resulting in some solid shots on Becky.

Coach wisely called a timeout. "Jackie is getting hammered in there, Coach," Sam said.

Coach looked at me. "What's going on?"

"It's nothing. They're just holding their ground," I said, not wanting to say how much I was getting pushed and shoved.

"Jackie, since you're getting a lot of pressure, switch with Tori inside the circle. If they stay with you, it could free up some space for the others to maneuver."

So I went back on the field thinking this was a pretty good plan. And if they got all over Tori, I might be able to slip in and tap the ball in myself.

There were just ten minutes left, and when Somerville's defense realized I wasn't going to goal, sure enough, they let me be and concentrated on clogging up the middle of the goal mouth. A moment later, when Tori and a Somerville player were battling for the ball, I slipped from behind Tori and moved toward the goalpost. All of a sudden the ball popped loose like it was on a mission to find my stick. Just as I was ready to sweep the ball into the cage a Somerville player came out of nowhere and shoved her stick into my ribs. A sharp pain went through my chest and I stumbled to the ground.

"Don't even think you're going to score on us, bitch," I heard someone say over me. I couldn't answer her back. I couldn't even breathe.

"Get Sam before she gets tossed out," someone said, and then a whistle blew.

I looked up just in time to see Jules stepping in between Sam and some kid from Somerville. Jules was pushing Sam away talking to her in a low voice all the while.

I rolled over on my side and could only think about the pain. The next thing I knew Coach was by my side talking to me. "Can you get up, Jackie?"

I stood with Coach's help, but as I straightened I let out a gasp and bent over. "Might have broken a rib," I heard the ref say to Coach. Our trainer joined Coach and the two of them helped me to the sidelines. I gingerly sat on the bench trying not to move any more than I had to while some of the other players went to get my sweat suit for me. I was starting to feel super cold.

"I gotta go back in, Coach," I said in a hoarse whisper.

"Not now, Jackie," she said, and patted my back.

I watched the rest of the game through a haze. The ref must have seen the Somerville player take me out 'cause she awarded our team a penalty stroke. It was our chance to finally score. Jules stepped to the line and sent a low blast into the corner of the cage. We were up 1-0 and that's how the game ended.

Afterwards Mrs. Hanson came up to me. "I called your dad and he's going to meet us at the hospital," she said. "You need to be checked out."

In the car Tori and Jules gave me the low-down as to what happened after I got hit. "Sam was going to deck that girl," Tori said excitedly. "Thank goodness Jules stepped in and calmed her down."

"Their coach came up to Coach after the game and apologized saying she hoped you'd be okay. She told Coach she was totally embarrassed," Jules added.

"The girl got tossed you know. Had to sit out the rest of the game. Bet she's in big trouble," Tori said.

"It was really ugly out there," Jules said. I didn't know Somerville was like that. Lindsay said it might have something to do with the hockey forum. She couldn't wait to see what was on there tonight," she said, shaking her head in disgust. "She's being stupid. It's just a bunch of gossip."

Is that really what today was about? The hockey forum? Sometimes I hated the Internet.

Dad was waiting for me when we got to the hospital. Then we had to sit there for almost two hours before we got X-rays. I was feeling miserable, and it was hard to get comfortable my chest was hurting so much.

Finally the doctor came back into the little room the nurse had stuck us in. "The good news is there is no break. However there is a lot of bruising and it is going to hurt to breathe for a while. You really need to rest and ice the area that is sore."

I looked at my dad wondering what the word rest really meant. He turned to the doctor, "My daughter's hockey team is making a run in the state tournament."

The doctor paused, making notes on his clipboard, and peered up at me through his rimless glasses that reminded me of Ms. Gillespie."Ice hockey already?"

"No," I sighed. *Why didn't everyone know the only hockey that mattered was played on grass?*

My dad interrupted. "She plays field hockey."

"Well, she needs to rest for a week, then maybe she can get back on the field. It depends on how she can handle the pain."

A week!!! This can't be happening.

The doctor went on, oblivious to the horror on my face. "She'll need to see her family physician before the school will let her play."

"No problem," my dad said, and shook the doctor's hand.

On the way out to the parking lot I grabbed my dad's arm. "Please don't tell Mom. I need to be out there."

"I'm not going to lie to your mother. If she had her way there would be no more hockey ever. She hates to see you get hurt."

My temper started to heat up. "That's not fair. Matt's gotten hurt plenty and she never stopped him from playing soccer."

My dad sighed at this obvious fact. "You have to understand. You mother grew up in an area where girls didn't play sports that much, only basketball or track. Besides, your mother was always working to save money for college, so she never had a chance to see the joy that playing gave the girls who were athletes.

"Well, I'm sorry, but it matters to me."

"I know," he said, as he beeped the car open and helped me get in. When he turned on the engine Dad turned to me and said, "I **do** know what it means, so as long as you follow doctor's orders I'll help you to get back on the field."

When we got home that night Mom was fluttering all over me. She tried to hug me, but trying to avoid the contact, I moved too quickly, and couldn't mask the pain that must have shown on my face. Before my mom could go off on a tirade about the dangers of sports, my dad stepped in, assuring her that I would be fine and just needed to take it easy for a while.

My mom's eyes narrowed and she looked me over like she was examining a head of lettuce for hidden damage. Then she apparently decided I would live, and said, "Your coach called asking about you and so did the twins. Better make some phone calls after you shower and get out of those clothes."

I looked to my dad hoping he was going to smooth things over. He gave a brief nod, so I turned and went upstairs. Washing away the smells of the hospital made me feel almost new, but as I leaned over to pick up the soap that had slipped out of my hand I saw stars. A searing pain crossed my chest. I couldn't deny it. I really was hurt.

I called Coach first assuring her that I was okay, it was just a bruise. The hard part was telling her what the doctor said. I was surprised she took it in stride saying there were plenty of games ahead for me as long as the team did what they should. That did make me feel a little better.

Next was the twins. Tori answered. "You won't believe what happened after you left. Kate called and filled us in."

At the mention of Kate's name I started to bristle, and then realized I was being ridiculous. It wasn't Kate that dug her stick into my ribs. I needed to accept that she was Jules' best friend now, and that was that.

Tori continued and seemed to be relishing in delivering the gossip almost as much as she probably did hearing it for the first time. "The girl admitted to her coach that she and her friends had been on the hockey forum since the season started and had first been surprised and then annoyed by the jacmcshootr character and what they wrote. Honestly, Jackie, that's what this was all about. They finally figured it was you bragging and dissing their team. They just got ticked. I think our whole team is checking it out tonight. I'd sure like to know who wrote this stuff."

I thought, *so would I, so would I.*

(19)

The next morning we were having a short practice as some of the seniors and Jules were taking the November's SATs. As we walked across the parking lot to the field, I asked Tori why she wasn't taking them, too. "Jules wants to settle on a college this year," she said. "She figures if she can get strong scores on the SATs, a good school might sign her now. Unofficially, of course."

I blinked in confusion with all these terms like 'official,' 'unofficial.' Before I could ask Tori what she meant, she said, "I'll take them later. What's really important is my art portfolio. Right now, Mr. Latta, my drawing teacher, is helping me put together my best work. It'll take all year, but I need to start sometime."

Is this what everyone is doing? Tori saw the worried expression on my face and laughed."Don't judge doing college stuff by me or Jules. First of all you know Jules always has to have everything lined up in life." I nodded knowingly. "And second, courses like art and music have special requirements. Even if you're smart, if you don't have talent they won't take you. "You weren't planning on a singing career, were you?" she said, as she threw her arm around me.

I thought back to my time at camp practicing for our skits. "No way," I said, and started to laugh, then grabbed my side. I had to remember no more laughing for a while.

"See," Tori said, as we stepped onto the field, "no problem then. You'll be fine."

We found the rest of the team gathered around the bleachers. There was a buzz in the air and it didn't seem to be about the day's practice. "I'm telling you someone called you guys a bunch of stuck-up snobs," our manager Brit said, as she began to fill our water bottles from the large can at the end of the bench.

"Yeah, and how about the comment that the only reason we got past Somerville was 'cause of a cheap penalty stroke," Lindsay said, reaching around Brit to snag a bottle before anyone else.

"Why does everyone hate us?" someone wailed. "What did **we** do?"

No one heard our coaches come up behind us. "Girls," said Mrs. Fortunata, "you're going on a run." Everyone groaned. "And then we're having a meeting in the gym."

It was hard just sitting on the bench while everyone else was together on the run. Even though running was the last thing I wanted to do with my sore ribs, it would have sure beat sitting on the bench by myself. It made me realize just how tough it must have been for Jules the first days of the season when she could do nothing while waiting for her ankle to heal.

Thirty-five minutes later everyone was sitting on the gym floor waiting for Coach to speak. "It's come to my attention that a number of high school players are participating on an Internet hockey forum." Everyone looked around surprised that Coach would bring it up. "Apparently," she went on, "some players took the comments on the site to heart and took out their frustrations on one of our players yesterday." I could feel my teammates' eyes boring into me making me even more uncomfortable than I already was sitting so still with the pain in my side.

"The point I'm trying to make," Coach said, "is not so much that someone used a tag that would suggest she was Jackie. And, Jackie, I was so sure even before I view the forum, that I didn't even need to ask."

I hadn't even thought about that, that Coach might think I would dis on another team. It got me even more upset with whoever had pretended to be me.

Hands on hips, Coach started pacing back and forth, a sure sign she was worked up. Then she suddenly stopped and faced us. "I have no time for people that use the anonymity of a website to put down anyone who plays our sport. Certainly we can be fans of a particular team, or admire an individual player, but negative comments disrespect the game you play and the players who work hard every day to be as good as they can be."

Players were beginning to squirm. I was sure some of my teammates had trash-talked on the forum, or at the very least, had enjoyed seeing other people being put down. I knew people vented all the time on other social networks. Some of the stuff they said might be true, but often it wasn't. How could anyone know the difference?

I watched Coach as she waited for her words to sink in, and I could tell whatever she said next was going to be important. "I've been lucky enough to win three state titles and have come close several others times," she said.

My eyes widened. It was the first time Coach had alluded to Northfield's previous championships.

"It is a very hard road," she said. "And to be honest, there is always a piece of luck picked up along the way if you make it to the top. However, the teams I coached that **did** go all the way had one thing in common."

You could hear a pin drop. We all wanted to know if maybe our team had whatever it was, too. Ms. Gillespie pulled over a freestanding chalk board next to Coach and handed her a marker.

Coach waited again for our attention, and then she said, "They did not let anything get in the way, nothing from the outside, and nothing on the inside."She could see some of us were a little puzzled, so she asked, "What would be an example of something on the outside that could get in our way?"

There was silence. "How about a bad call?" Coach said, trying to get us to open up. That got some of us nodding. Who hadn't sulked during a game because they thought they were getting ripped off by a bad call. Then someone raised their hand, "Doing bad in school!" There was a lot of clapping on that one. "Parents a pain." "Fight with the boyfriend." As the comments flew Coach wrote them on the left side of the blackboard. They were all right on target.

"Okay, this might be a little harder," Coach said, as she drew a line down the middle of the board which now had one side blank. "How about problems on the team itself?" No one raised their hand.

Finally Anna said, "I think we're all fine."

I thought of Lindsay and Jules. The thing was, although I knew they didn't like each other, their feelings never seemed to get in the way with how they played on the field. Then I considered Jules and Kate Carson. I had to get real with myself. I'd let my jealousy over their friendship get in the way of my focus on the field. Not all the time, but enough so I wasn't giving the team a hundred percent of me. I wondered, too, if Kate ever noticed my coolness toward her. And then of course there was Jules. Did I still matter to her? I was so wrapped up in these thoughts that I lost track of what Coach was saying. Suddenly someone was passing out paper and pencils to everyone.

I looked at the person next to me with a questioning expression on my face. She whispered, "We're to write down two things that get in our way either off or on the field. I looked at my teammates who were concentrating on what they were committing to paper. Did that mean they had issues, too? I thought I was the only one. I saw Tori looking at me and wondered if she was going to mention her dad, or maybe was she thinking about me and my problems with Jules. Had she guessed the real reason Jules and I weren't as close as before?

"When you're done I want you to write down these words," Coach said. "This is what is in my way of winning a state championship. Take the paper home and decide what you are willing to do or change to make it happen. If everyone can fix one thing, there is no stopping us."

I quickly scribbled down Kate and Jules. Everything else I thought I could pretty much take care of. At least that's what I thought.

When we got home from practice I taped the paper over my mom's 'to do' list, and when I went downstairs for lunch I found Dad and Lizzie were in the kitchen showing off a fourth grade craft project they had been working on to Mom.

"How's Grandma doing? I asked as I got some juice from the fridge.

"Good," Dad said. "Your mother and I talked. We plan to bring Grandma to our house for a while when she gets out. I don't want her alone just yet. Jackie. That means you're going to have to go back to sharing a room with Lizzie for a week or two."

Having Grandma well enough to be at our house was great news, and I high-fived my sister saying, "It'll be just like old times, Lizzie." I watched her eyes sparkled and realized that maybe she had missed me after I took over my brother's room last year more than she had ever let on.

"How are you feeling by the way?" Dad asked as I slid into a chair.

"Okay, I guess. I hate sitting though, and the cold air makes breathing hard." When I heard my mom's sharp intake of breath I could have bit my lip. I couldn't let on to her how crummy I was feeling or she'd never let me play again.

Dad glanced up at my mom, and then patted my hand, "It'll get easier each day, but it might be good to take a scarf and breathe through it if it stays cold."

I whispered a silent thanks to my dad taking some heat off my mom's ready objections that I knew had been on the tip of her tongue right then. It was going to be tricky over the next few days, I thought.

"Say Mom, could you call Dr. Bernstein Monday and make an appointment for me on Wednesday so I can be checked out?"

"We'll see," she said, which I guessed was all I was going to get right then. She set a bowl of homemade chicken soup in front of me and all of a sudden I realized how doing nothing for a few hours could still really make a person hungry.

I was wolfing down a second bowl when Mom said, "Feeling well enough to work at the theater tonight?"

I'd forgotten. I was supposed to be there at five o'clock. It was the last thing I wanted to do, but I knew if I whined about it Mom would take it to mean I was too hurt to play so I told her okay. It turned out I would have been better off staying home.

I was glad to discover I was working alongside Carla again that evening. She had a way of making everything go so smoothly. Around seven o'clock lines started to form for the seven-fifteen and seven-thirty shows. Carla had me busy working the fountain filling soda orders and getting popcorn while she handled the candy purchases and the cash register. We were really making a good team.

I was grabbing a bottle of water for her when I turned and stared into the startled eyes of Mitch Kennedy. If I had taken three steps I could have reached out and touched him. From the way his face paled I think he was as surprised as I was. I couldn't seem to make my feet move. When the drink order wasn't coming as quickly as expected, Carla turned with a look of impatience that was quickly replaced by a look of concern.

"Here," she said, reaching out to grab the bottle of water from me.

As Mitch handed her the money, he started to say, "Jackie ..."

Whatever words he would have said next I'd never know, as all of sudden Emma Connors appeared by his side and placing her hand on his shoulder pleaded in a phony little-girl voice, "I'm **so** thirsty. Will you buy me a diet coke?"

I didn't wait for his reply, but turned and grabbed a cup from the stack, and began to fill her drink, a 'small' of course. Why should she spend Mitch's money? I placed the drink on the counter and started to walk away.

Emma called out, "Thanks so much, Jackie."

She wanted me to turn and watch the two of them together all lovey-dovey. I wouldn't give her the satisfaction. Instead, I walked to the end of the concession stand and busied myself restacking popcorn boxes.

A moment later I heard Carla's voice behind me. "Whoever they were, they're gone. Are you all right?"

I turned and brushed away the tears threatening to roll down my checks. "Yeah, just give me a sec."

For the next ten minutes I kept myself as busy as possible and then the lines were gone.

The next movies wouldn't be starting for half an hour. "What the heck was that all about?" Carla asked.

"Old boyfriend. We haven't seen each other in over a year."

"Bad breakup hmmm?"

"No breakup exactly. We were fine, but he had to move back to Texas to live with his mom.

"Didn't you guys stay in touch?" Carla asked as she folded her arms and leaned back against the counter. She obviously didn't understand what happened and maybe I didn't either.

I shrugged my shoulders. It was hard to explain. "We emailed for a while, but then it just got too complicated. I missed him so much. I was a mess, and finally decided to just stop and get on with my life."

"Wow, so you cut him off, right?"

"I guess." I had never thought of it that way. I could see from her face that she really didn't understand. "Anyhow he's got a new girlfriend now. It's just she's such a beast."

Carla studied me for a minute. "Me thinks you're jealous and maybe still like him."

I glanced up to find a man waiting to give his order and gave Carla a gentle nudge. "Me thinks we've been talking way too long and need to take care of our customers."

That night I played our split-second connection over and over in my mind. His warm gray eyes, the way his dark hair couldn't seem to be controlled, were still the same. But his jaw line was harder with a hint of a shadow. He looked like someone who lived much longer than the year he had been away. What if Emma hadn't been there? What if we had met someplace else? Would things have been any different? Probably not, I thought, feeling my heart close in on itself for protection, and thought again, probably not.

(20)

On Monday I was surprised to see Anna sitting by herself at lunch. "Where's Will?" I asked, as I put my tray down.

"On a trip with the engineering club," she said. Then she looked around to see we were still alone. "Listen, we need to talk."

Surprised, I stopped munching on my pizza, wondering what was up.

"Will and I were at the movies Saturday night. I saw what happened," she said.

I nearly choked on the pizza's gooey cheese and had to gulp down a bunch of water. When I was settled, Anna went on. "When Will asked me out he said we would be meeting up with some of his friends. Jackie, you have to believe me, I didn't know one of them would be Mitch. I saw him go up to the counter where you were working and ..."

"Hey guys." I looked over my shoulder to see Noah and his girl approaching the table.

"Later," Anna whispered.

The rest of the afternoon my mind was filling in all the possible 'ands' — *and I couldn't believe Emma would slink up there with him, and he's only dating her because she's* *thrown herself at him, **and** Will told me Mitch doesn't really like her 'cause he's still in love with you.* I liked that one best.

When practice ended, and there still had been with no chance to talk with Anna, I was practically hyperventilating waiting for her to finish the conversation about Mitch. She finally caught up with me as I was walking back to the locker room. "I hope you aren't upset I couldn't give you a heads up at the movie theater. I was so surprised to see Mitch walk in with the others," she said.

I swallowed hard. I hated putting Anna in a tough spot, but I needed to say it. "So he's dating Emma, right?"

"That's it. I don't know. There was a gang of them that walked in at the same time, but I don't know if they came together or if Emma is trying to make it work that way. I can't ask Will. He's very closed off when it comes to Mitch. If you really want to know I could always tell you if I pick up on anything."

I waved the idea away. "No, that's okay. You should just enjoy being with Will. Don't worry about me."

She paused right before the door to the locker room and let some others walk by. "You still like him, don't you?"

I sighed. The whole talk was exhausting. "It doesn't matter," I said, as I pulled on the door handle and went inside.

*   *   *

The next day was the South Jersey Group Four Semi-final. We were traveling to another school in our conference who was playing host to the game between us and the shore area school that was our next opponent. It was beyond weird sitting on the bus in my sweat suit knowing I was not going to be taking one step onto the field that day. I felt like I was letting my teammates down, but knew until I saw a doctor I was stuck. Thank goodness my mom relented and scheduled a doctor's appointment for the next morning.

As I stood on the sidelines when the starting lineups were announced and watched the players jogging out onto the field, it felt like one of the worse moments of my life. I ached to be standing shoulder to shoulder with my teammates as the national anthem played. I vowed if they got through the game I'd be ready for the next one.

Surprising what should have been a challenging game was an easy one. We won 5-1. The whole team was fired up, and I easily got caught up in their happy spirits on the ride home knowing it wasn't over and I'd get another chance to play.

The next morning I snatched up the sports page a soon as my dad was done with it. I wanted to read about our game while I was sitting at the doctor's office. As soon as we got there the receptionist sent us right in. I figured she must be connected to the teaching staff at Northfield, and they all had made a deal not to let any students miss too much school. After Dr. Bernstein examined me, he told my mom he would write a release for me, but I was to take it easy and should wear a protective pad over my ribs. "Don't expect to be a hundred percent, young lady," he said, shaking a finger at me. I had known Dr. Bernstein since forever, and he knew I was always the kind of athlete that had to get back out on the field no matter what.

"Are you sure, Dr. Bernstein?" my mom asked as he escorted us to the door.

My mom's worrying was making me crazy. "He's sure," I snapped. I saw my mom's eyes narrow at my tone, so I backpedaled a little more softly and put my arm around her. "Don't worry, Mom. I'll be fine."

As Mom drove me to school I thumbed through the sports section to high school sports and found a big article about the game saying how we were peaking at just the right time which sure spelled trouble for our next opponents.

Before the practice got officially underway, there was a lot more talk about what was in the paper and some cocky comments started flying around the team about how we were going to take it all and win the South Jersey Championship. Then someone shouted, "Hey, that's nothing. We're going all the way!" Soon everybody was getting on board with the idea. I looked toward a scowling Jules. I didn't think she liked what she was hearing. Kate, on the other hand, seemed to be all into the talk herself. I smelled trouble.

It didn't take Coach long to pick up the over-confidence among the team. Going through the warm-up people were talking and laughing, not the way Coach liked a practice to start. Two minutes later the whistle blew. Coach told the goalies to take off their equipment and for the rest of us to get on the end line. Everyone groaned. They knew what that meant — suicides.

I lasted for three sprints and couldn't go any further. It was killing me to take such deep breaths. Coach called out for me to take it easy and try jogging around the outside of the field which pretty quickly turned into a walk. The rest of the team continued with the sprints for the next twenty-five minutes. Girls were leaning over, hands on their knees, gasping for air. Jules yelled at them to stand up and put their hands over their heads to get more oxygen, but they were beyond listening. It's not like the team didn't deserve it. They just didn't want to do it and acted like babies.

Finally it was over. Everyone congregated at the benches grabbing the bottles of water as soon as they were available. I looked over at Coach who was standing in the middle of the field, hands on hips, talking to Ms. Gillespie. She looked at her watch. She was not happy.

She whistled us over and told us to stretch. As she walked among us I could tell she was still seething. No one looked her way, either because they were too embarrassed about how we were fooling around, or because they were so mad at her for all the sprints. It felt like our team was at a crossroads, and one of our choices was to fold right then and let the next game be our last.

Finally Coach spoke. "Let me remind you. Nobody is giving us the next win. Once we get to this level anybody can beat anybody."

I heard some players muttering under their breath and became enraged. I was not having it and stood up. "Don't you remember what last year was like, everybody crying and the seniors a mess? That can be us in three days. I sure don't want to stop when we've come this far. Do you?"

I sat down in a huff, drained. My chest was killing me and there was nothing more I could say. Then Jules stood and asked if we could have a meeting without the coaches. Mrs. Fortunata checked her watch and said "okay," and that she and Ms. Gillespie would be on the bleachers **if** and when we were ready to practice for real.

"Jackie said it all," Jules said, when the coaches had left. "I remember last year, too. I can't believe the rest of you juniors and seniors have forgotten already. Lindsay raised her hand to speak and said how much she hated that day, and then a couple others said pretty much the same thing. Jules eventually wrapped up the meeting. "We all have other stuff on our minds and I know some of it is pretty important, but if we don't take care of what is in front of us, I think we'll all regret it someday," she said.

When practice resumed, it was all pretty quiet. I couldn't tell if what was said in the meeting was going to fix us or not. I guessed it was pretty much up to everyone to figure out how much the season really meant to them.

(21)

I could smell the lasagna cooking the minute I walked in the backdoor. Washing up at the sink, I wondered how the aroma of a person's favorite food baking in the oven could make the clouds from the afternoon disappear so quickly. Standing there, drying my hands, I began to feel the soreness from my first day back on the field. Not only my ribs, but my whole body was starting to ache. I couldn't believe that just one week away from practice could make such a difference.

I did my best to sit down at the table without showing any pain, however nothing slipped past Dad. "You feeling a little out of shape?" he said, smiling sympathetically.

The question made my mom spin around as she set the dish of lasagna next to my dad. "Anything wrong? Maybe you shouldn't have gone back so soon."

I sensed an inquisition building and I tried to head it off. "Nah, nah," I said. "Just a little stiff. I'll stretch tonight." My reply didn't seem to distract her from scanning my body with her X-ray 'mom vision' for any signs of additional cuts or bruising. I tried changing the subject. "Say, I didn't tell you guys. You know the girl that hit me? It was all about what some crazy person wrote on the Internet, and everyone from Somerville thought it was me who wrote it. I'd really like to get my hands on whoever sent that stuff.

"That's exactly why you're not to go on the Internet, Lizzie," Mom said, shaking her finger at my sister. "Jackie could have been seriously hurt because of someone's thoughtless acts."

My sister seemed to turn awfully pale all of a sudden and buried her hands in her lap. My Mom served dinner which was delish. As I got up for seconds I heard Lizzie say, "I don't feel good. Can I go to my room?" Without waiting to be excused, she got up from the table and raced upstairs.

"What's got into her?" I asked to no one in particular.

"I don't know," Mom said. "I'll go check on her in a little while. There's some flu going around at her school."

Later that evening I got a surprise phone call. It was Jules. "Hey, just wanted to say thanks for today. It meant a lot to have someone else put the team in its place."

"That's okay. I was really mad. We're **so** close."

"Great minds think alike. Seriously though ... we should talk."

Here it was, my moment to break the ice. I let out a long breath. "I agree. But let's not do it on the phone. Why don't we go do something together?"

"How about after the game?

"Uh-uh, gotta work Saturday." How about Sunday afternoon? Maybe we could go bowling."

"Yeah, right, something where height doesn't matter. Good way to level the playing field, Jack. I'll pick you up."

I chuckled at Jules' attempt to crank up the competitive nature that we shared. We could always do that with each other. It felt good.

Afterwards I realized she said she'd pick me up. I had almost forgotten she could drive now with only one other person in the car, and now it would be me. The thought of driving without an adult suddenly sounded so appealing that I couldn't wait for my Behind The Wheel Classes to start as soon as hockey was over.

*   *   *

The next morning I was scrounging through the cabinets for an energy bar when Mom came into the kitchen. "How's Lizzie? Is she going to school today?" I asked.

"When I checked her last night she didn't have a fever or sore throat. I was sure she was coming down with something," Mom said.

"Maybe she's PMSing," I said, biting into an apple-walnut bar.

"Jackie, don't even jest. Your sister's not even ten. I'm not ready to have her mature like that."

"She wouldn't be the first," I said. "I gotta say, I love Lizzie to death, but Matt and I decided a long time ago that she was going to make you and Dad crazy when she grew up someday."

"You both might be right. I just don't want it to be now."

I laughed and grabbed my backpack. As I opened the kitchen door to walk to the bus I said, "Hey Mom, maybe **you** should make a list. You know …. kind of 'what to do list' for a future with Lizzie as a teenager." I felt my mom's feeble attempt to hit me in the back with a kitchen towel as I walked out the door.

That night when I got home, I had some college mail and one was a letter from my parents' university. The coach wrote that she was hoping to see me play soon as she was making a trip to the East Coast to see some of her 'main recruits' and she was really hoping I would visit her school. *Was I a main recruit?* I wondered if she said that kind of thing to everyone just to be nice. It was kind of hard to tell. I decided I'd show the letter to my dad thinking it might make him happy with the legacy thing and all.

Later on I started clearing out my top bureau drawer for my Grandma to use when she came to our house from the cardiac care center. I was going back to my old room for a while, the one I had shared with Lizzie since she was a few weeks old.

I thought I had just about everything from the bureau drawer put into a box that I'd store in the back of my closet, when I took one final sweep reaching my hand into the far corners, and felt the tissue paper wrapped package from Mitch. I refused to let myself think about the past and quickly stuffed the package in the bottom of the box.

*   *   *

On Saturday, emotions were high as we piled onto the bus for the South Jersey Group Four Championship against Cherry Hill North. I reached inside my jacket pocket for the latest note that had been dropped into my hall locker the day before. I fingered the edges, but didn't take it out. I remembered every word.

You're a champion already!

The note felt like a good luck charm, like an extra player on the field or something. Remembering how much I had looked forward to finding the notes when they did appear, I was more determined than ever to find out the writer's identity. I wondered if I asked Dr. Howarth, our school principal, if I could install a surveillance camera above my locker, whether he'd let me do it.

The bus hadn't gone half a mile when there was a commotion a couple of seats behind me and all the excitement of our first South Jersey title game came screeching to a halt. Becky Weiss, our goalkeeper, was barfing all over her uniform.

Coach came to the back of the bus and helped Becky clean up. We all held our breath and hoped it was just nerves, but no such luck. Coach felt Becky's forehead, then flipped out her phone to call Becky's mom. It was the end of the afternoon for Becky. We all wondered if it was the end of the road for us, too.

The rest of the ride was quiet, each of us lost in our thoughts. Kerry Roth, the back-up goalie had some mighty big shoes to fill. Once we arrived at the field, and Becky's mom met the bus to take Becky home, we began our pre-game warmup. We couldn't help but steal glances at Kerry and our third-string goalie as they practiced their footwork and kicking drills with Ms. Gillespie. I could tell by our anxious expressions that we were all worried. Halfway through a very uninspiring warmup Jules called all of us field players into a huddle.

"Look, never mind the goalkeeping, either we have it or we don't," Jules said, sounding very frustrated.

Did we have it? I didn't know. I remembered how we had folded in the tournament a year ago when our captain, Mandy Stevenson, blew out her knee and couldn't continue playing. I was sure everyone else remembered it, too.

"We're all a year older," I said. "Maybe that means we're a lot tougher. I don't know for sure. But one thing I do know is … I'm not ready to turn in my uniform on Monday. Are any of you?"

That seemed to get everyone fired up. Then Anna said, "Our goalies have never let us down. Let's not let them down."

We did a cheer, then broke apart to finish our pre-game drills. As the whistle blew to start the game, I felt goose bumps spreading over my skin. Somehow I knew we were going to win.

The goal came just minutes into the game. Unfortunately it wasn't for us. It was off a super sweet corner play, two quick passes and then a long pass to the opposite side of the field, and Kerry couldn't get to it in time. To be honest, I don't think Becky could have either.

As we jogged back to the center to re-start play, our fans grew silent. I think they had lost faith. It was up to us. Either we could build a fire, or roll over and play dead. I was not giving up.

When the ref blew her whistle Sam sent the ball rocketing toward the corner of the field. But it was out of my reach, and a member of the other team came up with the ball. As she gathered it in, she looked into the area where she was going to hit the ball, and I knew what to do. Just as she struck the ball I took off into that space and intercepted her hit. Now she was the only one between me and the goalie. I did a little stick fake that left her in the dust and bore down on their goalkeeper. I don't even know what I did to beat her. I just knew I was going to put the ball in the cage and I did.

I barely turned around before I was enveloped in hugs, led at first by Sam and Tori, and then what seemed the whole hockey world. It was awesome. It was also very painful. Even with the cushioning the trainer had taped to my ribs, it felt like my ribs were on fire.

I signaled Coach to take me out and slowly moved to the sidelines, my hand holding my ribs. Watching from the bench, I could see the team's growing confidence right from the re-start.

They were swarming the ball so fast the other team couldn't seem to get it out of their defensive end. The energy continued into the halftime huddle. I could feel it bouncing off each of my teammates like a heat wave radiating out, surrounding every player on the team. I needed to be out there with them. I turned to Coach, "Please put me back in. I'm fine."

She gave me a long look, seeming to judge how 'all right' I really was. "Maybe after a bit," was all she said.

I started pacing on the sidelines as the minutes ticked down. *Put me in. Put me in.* I chanted in my mind. I knew to ask her again would only bring a 'no.'

With ten minutes left in the game I could see us starting to lose our edge. *No! No! No!* I shouted silently in my head. *This game isn't in the bag.*

My thoughts were the kiss of death. No sooner had I conjured them up in my mind than one of Cherry Hill's players stole the ball off of Heather's stick and sent a long pass to one of her attackers who was hovering near the edge of our striking circle. In the blink of an eye the ball was past Kerry and went into the cage. We were all tied up.

I stared at the back of Coach's head willing her to turn around and look at me. Finally, she called my name, and I raced to her side. "You sure you can do this?" I nodded. I knew she didn't want me in there, but she finally said, "Okay, report in."

I raced back to the bench to get my sweat suit off, my foot catching in the hem of my sweatpants taking my shoe with it. I sighed in frustration having to take time to retie my shoe while the clock was ticking down. I picked up my stick and almost forgot to grab my mouth guard. "Number two going in for sixteen," I said at the scorer's table, snatching up the substitution card and waving it at the girl who had replaced me. "Go get 'em Jackie," she said, as she grabbed the card from my hand.

In the closing minutes Jules came barreling down the field. At the top of the circle she sent me a crisp pass toward the end line. I cut in front of the player marking me and, with one long sweep, sent the ball where it belonged, in the back of the cage. This time my teammates were way more careful as they just fist pumped their congratulations making sure they stayed clear of my rib cage.

Lindsay called out, "The timer's up!" Sure enough, a manager with a clock in her hand was moving toward the ref, getting ready to count down the final seconds of the game. This made us bear down even more and we were closing in on a possible third goal as the whistle blew ending the game. Afterwards it was like freshman year all over again when we won our conference title, except this experience was magnified ten times over.

Kate and Jules poured a jug of water over Coach who took it in good stride. I guessed she was kind of expecting it since it was now her fifth South Jersey title. Families raced out on the field hugging their daughters and cameras were clicking away. In all the commotion I noticed Kerry slip away to the bench and pull out her cell phone. When she came back onto the field I asked her who she had called. "My buddy," she said. "I told Becky never to do this to me again or I'd have to stock up on senior citizen panty protectors."

"You didn't," I said.

"Yeah, I did," she said sheepishly. "The first time the ball came down the field." I gave her a hug and told her she was awesome, wet panties or not, and then we joined the rest of the team knowing that Becky was with us in spirit.

I saw a reporter start to make his way toward me, but Coach stepped into his path, said a few words, and sent him in Kerry's direction instead. I was both relieved for myself and glad for Kerry. She deserved to have a special moment of her own.

As the crowd thinned out and we made our way to the bus, I spotted Will walking with some other boys wearing Northfield jackets. I had to look twice to make sure I wasn't seeing things and nearly ran up Coach's back. But I knew what I saw — Mitch Kennedy had been at the game.

A few kids went home with their parents after the game, but most of us wanted to stay together and keep our winning buzz going. My dad, who'd been at the game, said he'd meet me back at the school. When we got back to school I slid into Dad's car and he said, "I noticed someone in the stands today wearing a jacket in my old college colors so I went up to the young woman and introduced myself. She was there to see you play, you know," he said, winking at me.

"But I hardly played," I said.

Dad paused for a moment as he was making a left hand turn, and then he said, "I guess it was enough."

I bit my lip and started to review the game in my head piece-by-piece, trying to figure out if what I did was good enough or if she had crossed me off her list. Then I remembered the name of the head coach that had signed the recruiting letter. "Was the lady's name Nancy Wright?"

"No, it was one of her assistants, Jody Daniels. I think the head coach is in Massachusetts right now."

I frowned. I guessed that meant I wasn't one of her 'main recruits.'

My dad must have read my thoughts 'cause he tapped me on the shoulder, "Don't worry. I think she must have liked what she saw because when she left she said she was relieved I came up to her." He saw my puzzled expression. "A coach can't initiate contact with a parent since you're only a junior."

"How do you know all this?"

"One of the many, many NCAA recruiting rules your mom and I had to learn when soccer coaches were looking at your brother." As we reached our house Dad said, "I already called your mother. You know she wished she could have been there, too, but she didn't want to leave your grandma alone just yet."

I nodded. I did understand. As I climbed up our steps, despite all my aches and pains, I could feel the afterglow of our great win. And, if I was honest, there was a part of me that was excited that Mitch was there. If anyone would know how much the game meant to me it would be him.

(22)

I slept late the next day, and when I woke, I was aching all over from the game. The South Jersey final had really done me in. For about two seconds I thought about blowing off my bowling date with Jules, but knew it was way too important to cancel.

Jules picked me up around two. It was so cool driving in the car, just the two of us. I felt totally free, like we were really on our own for the first time in our lives. Jules rattled on about the game which I was happy to do since there would be plenty of time 'to talk.' I also tried to focus on how Jules was handling the car. In just a couple of weeks my Behind The Wheel sessions would start. I had already been getting a little nervous about the class, but now I could see taking the class would be worth it.

At the bowling alley, when we went to the counter to pick out our shoes, the man there said, "The lanes are pretty open now. In another hour or so it'll start getting packed with the leagues, so you can't bowl too long."

"That's okay," Jules said, and it was fine by me too 'cause my ribs were killing me.

'What's with the kiddie ball?" Jules asked when she saw me returning from my ball search with a neon pink, eight-pound ball in my hands.

"Don't you worry about **my** choice of weapon," I said, trying to keep things light. "Let's see how many pins you can knock down with the monster you chose." She chuckled at my comment as she turned the sixteen-pound ball over and over in her hands. My eyes narrowed at the challenge.

"Age before beauty," I said, indicating she should go first. We traded turns for a few frames and then I knew it was time to open up the real topic of us being there.

"You all right?" Jules said, as she noticed me rubbing my side.

"A little sore," I said. She picked up her ball and turned to take her position on the alley. *Say it! Say it!* My mind exploded with my need to apologize, and my fear of not getting it right and making things worse. "Jules, there's something I need to say ..."

She stopped her move toward the pins and turned to look at me. My face must have looked awful 'cause she put her ball back on the rack and sat down next to me. She leaned back against the bench and stretched out her long legs. "I'm listening," she said finally.

"I've been jealous. Jealous of you and Kate," I said. Jules' eyes widened. "I guess I was so used to always expecting it to be you and me when it came to hockey that I felt a little lost."

Jules leaned forward putting her elbows on her knees and began to massage her hands like she really had to think hard about what she was going to say. Finally, she stopped, and turned to look at me. "At first I felt so responsible for the team when I got named a captain that I needed to make sure everything was good between Kate and me. You know, I didn't know her all that well. We had never hung out, but when I found out how nervous she was to be a captain ..." Now I was the one to be surprised and it must have showed.

"Jackie, who would want to be a captain after Mandy Stevenson?" Jules said. "She was so awesome. Everyone loved her. She always seemed to say the right thing. Kate knew she could never be as good."

"I had no idea."

"Of course not, but that's not the point. I found out after a while that I really liked Kate. She was a senior and was looking toward her future the same way I was. We have a lot in common."

I thought, *yeah, like brains and maturity.* I felt miserable.

She touched my arm and made me look at her. "This has nothing to do with you and me. You'll always be my close friend, the one that knows me best. You just can't be my only one."

The words were hard to hear, but the one thing I had always admired about Jules was her honesty.

"There are things that we have shared that no one else ever will, well, besides Tori," she said. "We need to be okay again."

I thought for a minute. Maybe friendships were more complicated than I thought. Maybe they weren't so constant. Maybe the ones that really lasted were more of an up and down, push and pull kind of thing. The idea would probably need some getting used to, but today was going to have to be a start.

I smiled at Jules and felt the wall that had been between us crumbling away. I fist bumped her. "More than okay," I said.

"Pinkie swear?" Jules asked extending her finger.

"Pinkie swear," I said, locking her finger in mine.

We finished the first game and Jules went to get a soda. The place was getting noisy and as I looked around I realized the guy at the desk had been right. The place really was filling up. When Jules came back she said, "Mitch isn't really with that horrible Emma Connors, is he?"

I frowned, wondering what had brought that on. "I'm pretty sure," I answered. "I've seen her a couple of times draped all over him. Why?"

"Lane one," she said, thumbing over her shoulder, and that's when I saw a whole crowd of kids from our school, and right in the middle of them were Mitch and Emma.

I quickly looked away as I didn't want to be caught out staring, but I'd seen enough. "I can't tell if she's really with him or not. I'm sure no expert," Jules said, as she picked up her ball. "If you want to know for sure isn't there someone you could ask?"

As Jules let the ball fly down the alley for a strike I thought of possible people. Will was out for sure, and I hated putting Anna in the middle of things when she and Will were just starting out being a couple.

When I told Jules my dilemma she said, "How about Tori? You know she's the social snoop of the universe. If anyone can find out who's with who at Northfield it's her.

I'd never thought of Tori and mulled over Jules' suggestion as I took my turn. The ball wound up in the gutter and I could hear Jules' low chuckle as I stood there hands on hips willing the ball to jump back onto the alley and save my score.

Jules' laughter was enough to get me back on focus. Now that we kind of worked things out I needed to bear down and beat her. The score was still close going into the ninth frame. Jules picked up her ball and then put it down again. It turned out she had something on her mind, too.

"James and I are meeting up tonight," she said. I smiled, imagining the two of them together. "Anyway," she went on, "I know you guys are good buddies and I was wondering if he ever said anything about us."

Now it was my turn to be honest, and I didn't think I was breaking any confidences when I said, "Just he said you guys are trying to figure stuff out."

She nodded. "I don't know what to do. Tori's answer is to hold onto him, but I'm not sure if it's the right thing to do."

"Well, does he still matter to you?"

"Yes, of course. It's not that. I think we've just run out of steam. I mean he's the only boy I've cared enough about that I'd wanted to be with. Maybe I'm just not the romantic type. I think he deserves someone who really wants all that 'mushy stuff' his band is always singing about." She leaned forward, elbows on her knees, and said in a low voice, "Is there something wrong with me?"

It was on the tip of my tongue to make the quick reply — the 'of course not.' Instead I gave it some thought. Mitch made me feel all breathy and made my heart beat like it was gearing up for a seizure. Apparently James didn't do the same for Jules. James was a great guy, of course. A lot of girls at school hoped he'd look their way. I guessed it all came down to chemistry and it wasn't there for Jules and James.

"Maybe he's just not the right one," I finally said.

She seemed to mull over what I said and then let out a long breath and started to get up. I could tell this must have been weighing on her mind for a long time, but for the moment my answer was all I could give her. We finished the last frame, Jules inching passed me by a few pins. As we made our way to the front desk to return our shoes Mitch was walking right toward us. When he saw us his eyes widened and a grin started to break out on his face, and then disappear when he saw me slow up.

"I didn't know you guys were here," he said.

When I didn't say anything Jules stepped into the silence. "Yeah, trying to get away from hockey for awhile. We've got a big week coming up.

"I heard. Congratulations." He eyed me. "Good luck. I know how much you want it." His eyes moved to include Jules, but I knew he was really speaking to me. How many conversations did we have when we were younger, I wondered, thinking about playing for the big one?

"We better get going," Jules said.

"Yeah, right," he said, but his eyes never left mine. Then Jules tugged at my coat and we were gone.

(23)

Monday morning's newspaper had an article about all the South Jersey teams playing in the state semi-finals the next day. There was a paragraph about our team which mentioned the defensive talents of Becky and Jules, and then asked the question, "Can any high school team stop Northfield's little dynamo, Jackie McKendry?" I frowned at the line. It made me feel like a giant spotlight had been directed at me. I didn't like it one bit.

Surprisingly, a different spotlight hit me in fourth period gym. I was changing for class when Emma Connors, who had pretty much ignored me since the semester began, walked up to me and said, "Congratulations on winning your game Saturday."

Surprised that she would even care, I started to thank her, but as she walked away she said, "Make sure a championship is the only thing you're going after."

I frowned. Did she see me as some kind of threat? It was ridiculous. Then I got mad that she would even think I was the kind of person that would stoop so low as to try to come between her and Mitch if they really were a couple. It reminded me that I needed to put Detective Tori Hanson on the trail to get some answers.

Anna came over to me as I was tying my sneakers. "What's with her royal highness? She nearly ran me over she was in such a tizzy," she said. "Emma Connors," Anna said when she saw my puzzled expression. "She looked like she was ready to explode."

I smiled at the image of Emma scattered into a million pieces, then shrugged. I didn't want to get into it with Anna, especially if she and Will would be spending any time with Mitch and Emma. "Come on," I said, "It's time to learn the cha-cha," referring to the first dance in our new gym unit called "Intro to Ballroom Dancing."

Ms. O'Donnell had us practice the steps to the cha-cha en masse, and then she had us partner up. Emma, of course, grabbed Kurt Evans. Since there were more girls than guys in the class, I was stuck with a girl from my Spanish class who had two left feet. It took all my athletic ability to stay in time with the music and still manage to avoid getting my feet trampled by my partner.

After class was over Emma sidled up to me as we walked toward the locker room. "Stuck dancing with a girl, I see. Guess the boys have finally realized you aren't all that," she smirked.

I remembered getting my nails done for the prom last year and how surprised Emma was when she walked into the salon and found out I was going with Chris Hanson. She had made a snarky remark then, too. It took all my willpower not to reach out and slap her. As I watched her retreat through the doorway I tried hard to figure what Mitch liked about her. Then I remembered the blond hair and killer body. I could only hope that someday he would see she wasn't worth it.

At lunch I couldn't be sure, but I thought I detected a curiosity in Will about me. Like he had me all figured out and all of a sudden he wasn't sure he had gotten it right. I would catch him watching me over the cover of his book. I looked at Anna to see if she was acting guilty about giving something away about my feelings for Mitch, but she seemed her old normal self. It was a puzzle.

In English we had another substitute and were given busywork to answer with a partner. Naturally James and I pulled our chairs together and began doing the assignment. When we were halfway through James laid down his pen. "I don't know whether she's told you or not. Jules and I have ended it."

So she did decide, I thought. I studied him for a moment trying to judge how he felt about it. "You're okay with it?"

"Yeah, I saw it coming for awhile. Your friend is a very special girl, you know. I feel really lucky we met. I guess I have to thank you and Tori for that."

I smiled remembering the time I dragged the twins with me to see James' band play after Mitch had left school, and I had felt the need to fill my lonely weekends with some new activities. At first I had thought he and Tori were going to get together, but it turned out the twin he was attracted to was Jules.

James picked up his pen again. "Who knows," he said, leaning back in his chair, "maybe there'll be a song somewhere in all of it. What do you think?"

"Oh, no," I said, putting my hands up laughing. "My song writing career is over."

As we proceeded with the next part of our assignment I felt he wasn't the only lucky one. Jules had been pretty darn lucky, too.

*   *   *

Before I got to the field, I spent what I hoped would be my final time in the after-school 'algebra for dummies' class. Mr. Hoffner was giving me a test to see if I was now up-to-date on all the material. I had to admit the sessions actually turned out to be a good thing. The only bad part was the time I missed from hockey. When I handed in the test Mr. Hoffner told me to wait and he'd mark it right away.

I checked my watch and started shifting back and forth from foot to foot, anxious to be out of there, but also curious to see how I did.

"Ms. McKendry," Mr. Hoffner said, beaming at me. "You've gotten yourself a ninety-five. Well done." I smiled. "I hope the time here wasn't too painful," he said, knowing full well it had been the last place I had wanted to be.

"Thanks for your help, Mr. Hoffner. Actually I do think I've finally gotten it."

"Good," he said. "And, Ms. McKendry," he said, as I started to leave, "I'm sure no one can stop Northfield's dynamo in anything she does once she puts her mind to it."

I glanced back over my shoulder, surprised. I didn't think my algebra teacher was the kind of person who even knew there was a sports section in a newspaper. Who knew?

When I raced out to practice I saw Becky was there and breathed a sigh of relief. While Kerry had done a great job getting us through the last game, Becky was one of the quickest athletes in our school, and I was glad she was back.

At the end of practice Coach called us together and reviewed our plans for the next day. We would be meeting the Central Jersey Group Four Champions at a neutral site near Princeton. When we found out the team was a Toms River school, Jules and I looked at each other remembering the All-American we had seen playing at my brother's college. She had been from Toms River. I sure hoped none of tomorrow's players were going to be as good as her 'cause she had been awesome.

When I got home, Grandma McKendry was in the kitchen bustling about helping my mom with dinner. "Grandma, you're looking great," I said, noticing she was no longer in her housecoat, and was instead in one of her many velour sweat suits. This one was a crazy purple. I think she had one for every day of the week.

"Honey, you can't keep a tough old woman like me down for long," she said.

"Just don't do too much," I said, concerned she might have a relapse.

"Stop being such a worrier," she said. "Your dad even got me a Northfield sweatshirt. I'm wearing it when I go to Saturday's game."

"But Grandma, we're playing tomorrow."

"Of course you are. But your father won't let me go to that one. So I'll just wait for the championship game."

"Oh Grandma, you're the best," I said, and wrapped my arms around her. *Wait 'til I tell the team what Grandma said. They'll love it. But I better wait 'til after we get through tomorrow.*

I had the bedroom to myself that night. The last few days Lizzie had been spending her time in Grandma's room or downstairs watching TV until it was her bedtime. I thought she was being considerate so I could get my school work done without interruptions. I thought wrong.

Around eight-thirty Grandma came into the room with Lizzie in tow. I could see my sister had been crying.

"What's wrong?" I asked, surprised at the unhappy look on my sister's face.

Grandma sat down on the edge of one of the twin beds pulling my sister down with her. "Jackie, Lizzie has something to tell you." My sister sat there looking at her shoes, not saying anything.

"Go on," Grandma said none too patiently, and prodded my sister with her elbow.

I was stunned. This was **so** not like my grandma.

"It was me," my sister said finally, "the one on the hockey forum. I'm sorry." Then she ran out of the room.

My sister! I couldn't believe it. "Why?" I said to Grandma.

"Your sister was fascinated with everything the kids talked about at her school. You know Facebook, Twitter. She wanted to be part of it. Be cool. Your Dad is so strict." She put her hand up, "I know, with good reason. Anyhow, when she found out about the hockey forum she got obsessed with it. You know how much she loves you. She just wanted to show you off and she didn't understand the consequences."

I felt my temper flaring and rubbed my side reminding me what my sister's foolishness had almost cost me. Maybe we wouldn't even have won the South Jersey title. Our run to states could have been stopped by a nine-year-old. "Do Mom and Dad know?" I said through clenched teeth.

"Not yet, but they're going to. Lizzie has been miserable since she found out why you got hurt, and finally confessed to me what she had done. I'm sorry, Jackie. You have a right to be upset." Her voice trailed off, and then she said, "Remember she's just a little girl."

Grandma got up and left the room. I guessed it was to tell my parents. I could feel the anger crawling over my skin. I couldn't think straight. I had warned Lizzie about being on the darn forum and she kept using it anyway. That she went against what I had said to her made me mad as much as anything. I knew she hadn't meant me any harm. I wasn't ready to forgive her, though, not by a long shot.

My sister didn't sleep in her room with me that night. I guessed she bunked in with my parents and was relieved. I didn't think I could be civil to her just then. The next morning I left for school while my parents were still upstairs getting ready for work. I didn't want to hear any excuses from them about Lizzie. I had an itch and beating the Toms River school was just the way to relieve it.

We were being dismissed for the game at the end of fifth period. Since I was missing lunch, I had packed a snack and hoped it would tide me over 'til after the game. I met up with Sam and then the two of us ran into Anna who was hurrying to the locker room hand-in-hand with Will. At the door Will gave Anna a hug wishing her luck and said he'd get to the game as soon as he could. I knew he'd be late. Games started so early at the end of the season that a lot of students missed them, but I hoped he could make it for Anna's sake.

The bus ride was unusually quiet. We were so close to the end. Just one more game and we'd be playing for the championship. It was like we could reach out and touch it.

I had run through practically every song on my latest playlist and had just checked my watch when the bus driver pulled over to the side of the road. *Uh-oh this isn't good.*

The fact that the bus was no longer moving seemed to rouse those who were sleeping, and now everyone was sitting up in their seats looking around trying to figure out what was going on. We could see Coach talking with the driver and him shaking his head. Then the driver picked up his phone and made a call. We all watched as Coach made a call as well.

The team was starting to be anxious. "What was going on? Are we going to be late? What about our warmup?" The questions mounted. After her phone call was over, Coach had a whispered conference with Kate and Jules while the rest of us played detective looking for clues as to what all this meant. Finally Coach stood up. "There are some problems with the bus overheating. They're getting another bus to take us the rest of the way and it'll be here shortly."

Shortly? What did that mean? I looked at my watch again. It was almost one. We needed to be on the field. The game started at two. The minutes ticked by and we were getting more jittery by the minute. I could see our chance for a championship being washed away due to a stupid bus engine.

There was some stirring behind me, and then Becky, wearing her goalie helmet, was marching toward the front of the bus, with Kerry right behind her. "We were going to save this for our end of the season party," she said, "but we decided to do it now. We need the front two seats, so coaches, captains, you need to get to the back of the bus where you belong."

Everyone gave a little cheer at Becky's comment. Even Mrs. Fortunata had a smile on her face as she played along with Becky's instructions leading the others toward the back. "Kerry and I have made up a little song we want you to learn and then we're all going to sing it together," Becky said. A few players groaned. "Groaners will be thrown off the bus," Becky said. "This is your official warning." Everyone laughed.

"It's to *Row, Row, Row Your Boat*. Everyone knows that tune, right?" Becky asked. People started to clap. Then Becky and Kerry proceeded to teach us the words. They had made up two verses that poked fun of our coaches and the team. It was hilarious. Pretty soon everyone knew the words.

"Here's the hard part," Kerry said. "My side of the bus is going to start it and on Becky's signal her side will join in."

After a couple of false starts we finally got it. And we were going through the song for a second time when our rescue bus pulled up behind us.

After we changed over to the 'good' bus, Coach told us the opposing team and officials knew there had been a problem, so the game would start a little later. We just weren't going to have our usual warmup time. Then she told the goalies to start getting dressed as we'd be there in fifteen.

When we got to the school we just about knocked each other over to get out of the bus and be the first ones to the bathrooms. It had been way too long a ride. The officials only allowed us twenty minutes to get ready for the game. It wasn't much and Becky barely had any touches on the ball which would have been enough to get any team all crazed with worry.

As we stood out on the field for the national anthem and I looked out toward the line of spectators, it seemed a very small crowd compared to our last game. I guessed it was because most parents couldn't get out of their jobs for a game so far away. In a way it made the afternoon seem just like any regular old game instead of a state semi-final. I was thinking maybe that was a good thing 'cause we had been way too nervous on the bus.

As we huddled up before the opening whistle, I tried to get my feelers out trying to sense our readiness to play. I think Coach was doing the same thing. Then Jules said, "Nothing is standing in my way of a state championship. Pass it on," and she nudged the player next to her. At first the player didn't quite get it, and then she did. "Nothing is standing in **my** way of a state championship. Pass it on," she said, and turned and looked at the player next to her. And so the message went around the whole team.

We took the field as one. One heart and one mind. The game was ours right from the first whistle. Maybe the other team had an off-day. Maybe they had warmed up too long waiting for us. But I didn't think any of those things mattered. The game was meant to be ours.

After we won and we were heading to the bus, I saw Will walking to the end of the field waiting for Anna. He congratulated us both on the game, and then whispered something to Anna that had her blushing. She handed him her stick bag and as they walked toward the bus she leaned into him, their mutual attraction obvious to everyone around them.

I wondered if Will had come by himself and looked back at the fans slowly making their way across the field. Then I saw him. Mitch Kennedy had come to our game, and for the life of me I couldn't understand why.

(24)

At lunch the next day the table was still feeling the high from our state semi-final game. I was dying to ask Will about Mitch being there, but couldn't figure how to make the question seem a casual one. Sam saved the day when she leaned across Anna and said to Will, "Glad you could at least make it to the second half.

"Yeah, I didn't think I could go to the game at all, then Mitch said he'd take me." Realizing what he'd said, he glanced across at me and added, "Uh … he owed me a favor."

So that was it. Mitch hadn't been interested in the game, just helping out his friend. I should have known. I wasn't sure if I was more disappointed he wasn't there to see **me** play, or relieved that Emma didn't have anything to worry about and wouldn't bug me anymore.

In study hall, as I was reading a passage in my Spanish book, I thought about what Will had said about Mitch driving him to the game. I re-imagined the scene with me in the car sitting next to Mitch, instead of Will, both of us having a kind of 'into the sunset kind of moment.'

It brought a smile to my face just thinking about it. Then I wondered how impossible it would be to ever make up for the year that we lost, and the image broke apart, replaced by one of Emma nestling into Mitch so close that they looked like one person. I slammed my Spanish book shut so loud that it made the study hall teacher look up and a bunch of people turn around. I slunk down in my seat, wishing I could be invisible, and that Emma Connors would simply disappear.

We weren't having a regular practice that day. Instead Coach called for a team meeting. I think she realized our bodies could use a rest if we were going to be ready for Saturday's state final. Besides that, we needed to make plans for the team psych dinner we were having at Kate's house. After the South Jersey finals, all the parents had wanted to host a big celebration party at the new VFW Post in town, but Coach nixed the idea telling the parents to wait until it was all over, which led to a lot of grumbling from some of the parents. I guessed a person had to have a pretty thick skin to be a coach, and pictured future myself, with a whistle in one hand and a box of tissues in the other, as I waited for someone to jump down my throat about something.

* * *

The next morning as I was putting my jacket in my locker, when I turned around Mitch Kennedy was walking in my direction. I figured he would just pass me by, so I leaned against my locker leaving as much room as possible between us in the crowded hallway. Instead, he stepped right up to me like I had been his objective all along.

"Jackie, I'm glad I caught you."

He was so close I could barely breathe. I searched for some response, but every brain cell in my head had scattered to the far corners of the hallway.

"It's been a long time," he said, his gray eyes searching my face for I didn't know what. "Good game Tuesday. You must be excited about the finals."

Some mental activity finally kicked in, and I said in a hesitant voice, "Yeah, thanks."

Someone bumped into him which brought him even closer, and I felt myself lean toward him. *Please, please, please put your arms around me and say that everything can be okay between us once again.* Almost as if it had a will of its own, his hand reached out and gently tugged the end of my ponytail. "New addition, I see," he said in a quiet voice.

It suddenly dawned on me that he had only known me with my short curls. It just went to show how much had happened since I had last seen him. I turned my head and his hand dropped away to rest against my locker.

It was getting hard to stand within inches of him and not curl into him like I used to. That he probably belonged to someone else made the moment a misery. "Gotta go," I said at last, and started to duck under his arm.

"Can I call you sometime?" he said.

I pretended not to hear, and started to move away. I took a few more steps, then stopped. Mom had told me a long time ago that life was about taking chances and to follow what was in my heart. I wouldn't try to get him back, not if he was with Emma, but clearing the air about everything that went on after we parted last year was probably the right thing to do.

I turned back, dodged around a few people, and managed to grab hold of his arm. "Yes," I said, looking up at him. "I'd like that."

He smiled that wonderful infectious smile of his that made the whole world light up. My world at least. Then I turned and floated down the hallway to my homeroom.

*   *   *

At the end of practice I drew Tori away from the others and said, "I need your help."

She looked surprised, and then grinned at me, "Men?"

I rolled my eyes, "Is there anything else with you?"

"Not really. Call me tonight. We can discuss."

That night Lizzie walked into the room just as I was punching in Tori's number. "I'm on the phone," I snapped at her, and she turned on her heels and ran down the hall. I still had not forgiven her for all the nonsense on the Internet. I knew by now that Grandma had told my mom and dad and that Lizzie was being punished. But that didn't really matter. I just couldn't get over how she had broken her promise to me.

"So," said Tori, when she answered her phone.

"Okay. I need the scoop on whether or not Mitch and Emma Connors are a couple."

"And are you sure that he's still the one that makes your heart go boom-ka-boom?"

"Yes, why? Is that a bad thing?"

"No. Not really. Anyway it's not who you start out with, it's who you end up with that really matters," she said.

I kind of chuckled to myself wondering where Tori came up with a line like that. *Probably in a movie.* Sometimes Tori's over-romantic views were a little out there. "Seriously," I continued, "You'll check it out for me, quiet-like, right?"

"No problem, buddy. I hope I can dig up some dirt on Emma while I'm at it. She totally needs to be removed from the upper echelon of Northfield society."

I laughed. "You are special, Tori."

"You bet I am," she said.

After the call ended I tried to get back to my schoolwork, but within a few minutes I was interrupted by Grandma coming into the room, and she motioned me to sit next to her. "Jackie, we need to have a talk."

I took a seat beside her, puzzled. *What would we possibly need to talk about?"*

"I think the thing between you and your sister has gone on long enough," she said.

"What do you mean?"All of a sudden I felt like I was the one in trouble instead of my bratty sister which was ridiculous.

"I know your sister disobeyed your parents' rules about the Internet and her actions directly affected you. But deep in your heart you know she never meant anything to happen to you.

I frowned, and wondered if Lizzie was behind this, and if she had gone and batted her big blue eyes and whined to Grandma that I wasn't being nice. It would be just like the little monster 'cause she had always been such an expert getting her way with Mom and Dad. I studied Grandma's face and debated what to say.

Grandma filled in my silence by patting my arm. "Life's too short to hold on to all that negative energy. Besides," she said, with a twinkle in her eye, "you need all your strength for the big game."

That made me smile. Grandma was one smart woman, maybe way too smart not to see through Lizzie's little acts.

"Oh, Grandma," I said, leaning against her shoulder. "I told her to stay off that forum, but she didn't listen."

"Jackie, we McKendry women can be a stubborn lot. Believe me, I've made my share of mistakes in life because of my stubbornness. Some I regret to this day."

I thought of my grandma lying in a hospital bed thinking about stuff she was sorry about, that maybe she couldn't fix anymore. "Okay, Grandma. I'll talk to her."

"Good girl. She's in your bedroom reading."

I stood in the doorway watching my sister sitting on the floor next to my bed. I didn't think she knew I was there. Tears were rolling down her face onto her book. I felt myself cave and slid down beside her. "What're you reading?" I asked.

My sister looked up at me, and I could see her misery. "Jackie, I'm so sorry. I promise never to use a computer again."

I reached over and tucked a lock of her hair behind her ear. "You don't have to go that far."

"Yes I do. Mom and Dad said so."

I smiled. "Maybe for right now, but they'll change their mind eventually. You just have to be smarter about things. For everything good about the Internet, there can be a few bad things, too. Saying stuff about people is just one of them. Better not to say anything at all sometimes.

She nodded. "I love you, Jackie."

I hugged her. "Me too, kiddo. Me too."

*   *   *

Friday evening I grabbed the bowl of pasta salad that Grandma made for the team dinner and hurried out to the Hanson's waiting car. I slipped into the back and for once in a really long time felt perfectly happy and relaxed to be sitting next to my old friend Jules, or at least pretty relaxed, since Tori was driving under the watchful eye of her dad. This time he didn't yell, probably because winning a game wasn't involved.

Kate's house was in a development similar to mine. It was like some architect guy had an idea of what a neighborhood should look like back in the eighties, and then copied the look all over South Jersey. When I walked into Kate's house it was like I could tell where every room was without ever having been there before. Tori needed to use the bathroom, and I told her to walk down the hall and make a right. When she came back she said, "How'd you know that?"

"Telepathy," I said, thinking of a word on my vocabulary list.

Jules rolled her eyes. "Tori, the house is just like Jackie's."

Someone called "Dinner's ready," and suddenly there was a massive charge to the Carson's kitchen. Food was always serious business. After we gorged ourselves and cleaned up, we all congregated back in the Carson's family room feeling relaxed and satisfied. Then Coach called for order, "Girls, we need to talk about tomorrow." We all sat up a little straighter. The only sound was the distant chatter of a few parents talking in the kitchen. "It's been several years since a Northfield team has been to the Group Four Finals, and if any team deserves to be there it's you." We all cheered and fist pumped the air.

When it quieted down again, Coach went on. "Sometimes when teams find themselves playing for a championship they forget about the game and get themselves caught up in all the hoopla. Then the only thing they think about is winning or losing a title. When they think like that the results are rarely good ones.

We were stiller than still, listening to what Coach was saying, trying to digest her words. "Newspaper articles, well-meaning parents and friends, the Internet," she said, as she went on, "can all get in our way of remembering it's still just a game, a game of hitting a ball into the goal cage more times than the other team does. When you're out there tomorrow I want you to remember that."

I nodded and saw others smiling. They had gotten it, too.

When I got home I turned on my cell and realized I had a message. It was from Mitch wishing me luck in the game and saying he was bringing Will and would see me there. For a second I regretted going to the team dinner and missing his call, and then remembered he probably belonged to someone else and was just being nice, sort of an athlete to fellow athlete kind of thing.

(25)

By the next morning the weather had turned raw and gray. I figured it was going to take a lot of layers for our fans to stay warm. Grandma was still insisting on going to the game and I was worried that maybe the cold air would be too much. But Grandma was pretty tough and said she wouldn't miss it for the world and only wished they had something like that when she played sports.

I remembered a long time ago she had told me she played some basketball in high school. "In the old days we only could run half the court," she had said. "They thought it would mess us up being female if we worked up too much of a sweat."

As I packed my bag for the bus trip, I shook my head recollecting Grandma's words about all the older ladies my grandma's age, and how lucky my teammates and I were to be having a big day like this. *This one is going to be for you, Grandma,* I thought, zipping up the bag, *and for all the other ladies, too.*

All four of the state games were being played at the same site, one of the New Jersey colleges that had turf. We were lucky the Group Four game wasn't scheduled 'til two o'clock which meant I could take my time getting ready for the game. When Dad dropped me off at the school, our bus was already there. One look told me that some of my teammates had been mighty busy. Handmade signs filled every window of the bus, plus someone had attached a huge blue and white banner along one side that read *Go Vikings.* I was pumped.

As our old yellow bus rolled past the toll booth, Coach called out that we'd reach the school in ten more minutes. Suddenly there was a burst of activity — one more look in the mirror, a check for loose hair braids, and finally all cell phones put in sleep mode. Then there was an awful silence.

Despite the cold seeping through the walls of the bus, I could sense perspiration start to build inside my shirt and had an urgent need to pee. I tried to relax by reading the psych signs the sophomores had taped to the windows, but the letters swam in my vision.

Then I saw Tori, who was sitting across the aisle, reach under her seat for her hockey stick, and began tapping it on the side of the bus and chanting. "We are Northfield and couldn't be prouder. If you can't hear us we'll yell a little louder." Her chant was soft at first, and then Becky joined in, then Lindsay and Anna. It finally got me going, too. By the time we pulled up to the field the noise was making the old bus shake with our power. And, as we gathered up our equipment and made our way toward the front of the bus, we were on fire. It was definitely going to be a good day.

The Group Two game was still going on, so a tournament administrator met us at the bus and escorted us to a locker room. Sitting there, waiting for the administrator to say we could go onto the field, it got quiet again. Everything we needed to say to each other had already been said. Even the coaches were silent. We all just wanted to go out there and play.

The moments ticked by and then the state administrator came back into the locker room and said the Group Two game had gone into overtime, so it would be at least another fifteen minutes. We groaned. I leaned back against the locker and closed my eyes. I tried to imagine what lay ahead — the march out to the field, our names being announced, and then listening to the national anthem. I felt goose bumps forming on my skin, and my mind raced to the end with us winning the game. What would happen then, a team-run around the track which surrounded the field, like they did in the Olympics? Would we all hold the trophy? Then my imagination ran out of steam, and I wondered for a minute if that meant we weren't going to win if I couldn't even picture what it would be like. I started biting my nails. I wished the clock would spin faster and the game was over. Suddenly I was scared.

After what seemed like forever, Ms. Gillespie came down the aisles, and told us we would be leaving in two minutes and "if anyone needed to use the bathroom to do it now." Half the team made a beeline for the stalls. Even though I didn't go, I could feel my stomach tying up in knots. I stood up and made my way toward the door. This was it.

As we exited the building we could hear the cheers of the winning Group Two school in the stadium. We knew somebody just had their dreams come true while another team was now in misery.

Coming out another door was a team dressed in black from head to toe. It was our opponents, Millbridge High.

"Holy cow, look at Millbridge," I head Lindsay say to Becky. "They're huge."

And they were. Five or six of them looked like they were as tall as the twins. They had won the state title for the last two years, and if looks had anything to do with winning, I could see why. They had run through all the competition from the north end of the state and so far had remained undefeated. The newspapers said they were the odds-on favorite to win it again this year. But I remembered what Coach said about not taking newspaper stuff too much to heart and decided that maybe today their streak was going to end.

Our two teams were now lined just a few yards apart near the entrance to the stadium. I was so busy with my plotting on how to beat Millbridge that I walked up Anna's heels and she let out a yelp. A few of the Millbridge girls noticed and burst out laughing at my klutziness. I was mortified. To make matters worse our lines were slowed down by the fans from the last game exiting the stadium, so there was plenty of time for all of Millbridge to have a good laugh at my expense.

As we were waiting in line to go in, I heard someone call. "Jackie, Jackie over here." It was Lizzie who was standing with my dad waiting to buy tickets for the game. She waved, then tapped a big, balding guy wearing a Millbridge sweatshirt who was standing behind her. "That's my sister," she exclaimed so everyone could hear. She was being kind of cute, I admit, until she said, "She's going to score a ton of goals today."

The man laughed good-naturedly, but I saw a couple of Millbridge players flashing me evil looks, and all at once I felt like my sister had once again painted a big target across my back. I muttered under my breath at my sister's nonsense. Then Jules who was right behind me said, "Hey, don't worry about what Lizzie said. Millbridge already knows you're our high scorer. They probably had someone at our last game. And besides, they've too much on the line to risk having one of their players getting tossed out of the game for unsportsmanlike behavior."

I thought about what Jules had said while we warmed up, and decided she was right. Once I came to that conclusion, I couldn't wait for the game to start.

Millbridge won the coin toss and elected to start with the ball in the second half. That meant we had to take the ball first to start the game. I figured they were expecting Sam to send the ball to the corners of the field like she usually did, so before the opening whistle I went over to her and suggested she do a little back pass to Heather instead. It worked and we were able to slowly inch our way down the field.

It was our last sustained possession for the next fifteen minutes. Every time we got the ball back Millbridge's big defensive backs used their reach to block up our passes. We started to get frustrated. On top of that they had one of their players shadowing me everywhere I went. She was watching me so closely I thought she could count every freckle across the bridge of my nose.

Times when I could double cut and get open, she would grab my shirt or hit my stick, so I couldn't get a touch on the ball. She was very subtle about it, though, and the officials weren't picking up on it. I was thinking maybe she was trying to get me fired up so I would be the one to get thrown out of the game, and, a year ago, I might have lost my cool 'cause I did have a bit of a temper. But what the girl didn't know was, I respected Coach too much to really get into it with another player. I just needed to figure out a way to beat the girl at her own game.

Just before the half ended Millbridge had a bunch of shots on Becky, one right after another. Becky got caught bumping into one of their rushing players going for the ball, and fell. The player shot, and as Becky attempted to reach the ball with her gloved hand, some player must have pushed her, 'cause Becky's stick dropped out of her hand. The official paused for a second and then blew her whistle. We all knew what it meant. A goalie can never play the ball without her stick in her hand, so it was a big foul against Becky. There would be a penalty stroke, an almost certain goal.

The official marched off the seven yards from the goal line and placed the ball on a small dot. A player from Millbridge came to the spot and on the official's whistle sent a well-placed shot into the corner of the cage. We were down 0-1.

We came off the field at halftime feeling like the game was slipping away from us. Coach was very calm and upbeat which kind of surprised me. I thought she'd rip us up and down. As she was giving us our final instructions I glanced over at the crowd and saw a bunch of guys in Northfield jackets and one of them was frantically trying to get my attention. It was Mitch and he was definitely trying to signal me. "What?" I mouthed silently and frowned. He kept holding up four fingers and then made a talking motion with his hands. I shrugged my shoulders and gave him a helpless look. I just didn't get it.

The whistle blew ending halftime, and as we huddled in for a cheer I was still clueless about what Mitch had been motioning about. As the minutes in the second half ticked by I kept trying to puzzle out what Mitch had been trying to tell me. All of a sudden Heather intercepted a careless pass and countered with a quick outlet pass to Cassie who took off down the field. As she neared the striking circle, in a rush to get the ball off, she mishit the ball, and it only went a few inches. Then she quickly hit it again. It was just one of those flubs that sometimes happens, but it threw off the timing of the waiting Millbridge defender, and Sam rushed in and got a piece of the ball, tipping it into the cage.

The goal got our fans off their feet, and in a blink of an eye, a lucky mishit evened up the score. As I jogged back to the center for the restart I had a chance to really notice the girl who was guarding me. She was wearing the number four.

The whistle blew and Millbridge had the ball. While our defense was busy keeping them out of our circle, I looked at number four again. She was staring at me like her life depended on it. *Four, talk, four, talk, what are you saying Mitch?*

All at once it hit me and I began ... "So ... I didn't catch your name? I'm Jackie. You a senior? My old boyfriend is standing over there. See him? The tall one in the blue jacket. He's got someone new. Bummers, right?" On and on I went. She didn't know whether to answer me or not, and it really didn't matter. I just kept right on talking. I probably said more to her than all of my opponents combined since the time I first picked up a stick in fifth grade. My chattiness must have gone on for ten minute or more. My mouth was getting dry from talking so much, and half the time it just sounded like a bunch of mumbles 'cause of my mouth guard. I could see she was starting to lose her concentration and I was beginning to get a step on her. I was biding my time for the right moment.

I didn't have long to wait. Jules intercepted a pass and was charging down the field. No one was picking her up, and I didn't blame them, 'cause Jules had that fire in her eyes that players have when they know they can't be beaten. I drifted off toward the side of the field, still keeping up my chatter to number four. She was just about to finally answer one of my questions, when out of the corner of my eye I saw Jules peek in my direction and start to bring her stick back.

It was like a signal, one that two players have who have played together forever always sense. It was all I needed. I stutter-stepped right toward number four, then rolled off of her and took off toward the top of the circle. Jules struck the ball. It was a perfect pass and I picked it up in mid-stride. I slammed it home and barely heard the whistle signaling goal when my teammates pounded my back and danced around me.

Jules rushed up and fist bumped me. "Nice going, there, number two."

"Not bad yourself, thirty-five," I said, slapping her on the back.

This was my dream I thought as I jogged back for the restart. The dream I had ever since I was a little kid. It had always been the same one. I was getting ready to score the winning goal, and then I'd wake up, or the dream would change into something else. I always wondered if it meant that I really didn't have it in me to score a goal when everything was on the line, and now I had my answer. I did.

The last three minutes of the game seemed to take forever. Both teams took the ball from one goal line to the other as each tried valiantly to have the game go their way, but in the end it was Northfield that prevailed. There were no words to describe how good it felt when that final whistle blew and we were crowned Group Four State Champions. I think it was everything an athlete could ever want.

The celebration went by so fast I could only remember a few things — the smile on Coach's face as she came out to meet us on the field, the formal presentation of the trophy to Kate and Jules, and posing for what seemed to me a million pictures, smiling so much I thought the muscles in my face would never be the same.

When things quieted down some I hurried over to Grandma, who was still sitting in the bleachers wrapped up in a blanket which seemed to cover her whole body."Whatcha think, Grandma?"

Her blue eyes were dancing and her cheeks were so pink it was hard to believe she was just getting over a heart attack. She grabbed my hand. "It was wonderful, honey. I wouldn't have missed this for the world."

I climbed back down the bleachers to join my friends, happy that my Grandma was alive and that I had helped give her such a fun day. As we moved toward the bus, I looked around the crowd exiting the stadium to see if I could find Mitch. I wanted to thank him for his suggestion of talking the Millbridge player to death 'cause it sure worked, but in all the craziness I had missed him. It was the only thing marring that once-in-a-lifetime day.

(26)

That night, in a state of happy exhaustion from all the celebration, I finally had a few moments to myself and decided to check my email. I didn't know how they found out so fast, but three college coaches had already sent their congratulations to me and hoped "I was still considering their school."

It was then that I heard the distant ringing of my cell. It seemed to be coming from the bedroom that Grandma was using. I raced down the hall and found my backpack tossed on the closet floor. I quickly emptied the contents on the bed and snatched up the phone.

"Hello," I said breathlessly, hoping it wasn't too late.

"Hi, Reds," a deep male voice said.

I caught my breath and flopped down against the closet door, my heart shifting into overdrive, and my brain becoming a jumbled mess. Only one person called me Reds. Mitch Kennedy. I tried to get a grip and think. Fortunately, he immediately started congratulating me on the game.

The game. An easy topic, thank goodness, I thought, and thanked him for his help with number four.

"It happens all the time on the basketball court. I thought it might work for you. I saw your grandma. Glad she's feeling better."

Another safe topic. I can do this. I can get through this phone call. But after a few more subjects were covered like school and mutual friends, I ran out of things to say, and grew increasingly nervous. And we weren't hitting on subjects that really mattered, like why he hadn't called when he first came back, what went on in Texas, and his relationship with Emma.

"Well, thanks for calling ..." I was starting to say goodbye when he interrupted.

"So, Reds, I was wondering if we could meet up, maybe at the library. What are you doing tomorrow afternoon?" I hesitated not knowing what his invitation meant, and then he said, "There are some things I'd rather talk to you about face-to-face."

"Oh, okay, I guess."

"I'll pick you up at two."

After the call ended, my mind began to race. *He's picking me up! That means in his car. Is this a date? No! He probably just wants to explain about Emma. Maybe he even wants to call me out for stopping the emailing last year.* I thought about phoning him back and cancelling. I didn't. But the phone call sure doused some water on what had been a perfect day.

*   *   *

The next day I must have stood in front of my closet for an hour discarding ideas on what to wear to my 'library meeting' with Mitch. That's what I called it when Grandma came in and found me, my clothes scattered over the floor.

"Isn't that the boy you dated last year?" she asked, sitting on the bed. "What ever happened to him?"

I kept my back to Grandma. "Yes," I said, pretending to study my clothes. "He moved to Texas."

"And now he's back and you're ... what do you call it nowadays, hooking up again?"

I whirled around. "No Grandma, we're not anything," I practically shouted. Then I remembered who I was talking to, and said more calmly, "We're just catching up. He's with someone else now."

"I see," said Grandma. She stood up and approached the closet. "Well let's see what we can find as the perfect 'catching-up' outfit."

My Grandma ... she always knew a lot more than she ever let on.

Within minutes Grandma had me subtly made up, in my best jeans and a fitted navy shirt. She turned me around, and decided that I was looking pretty hot without seeming to have tried at all, which was perfect. I gave her a hug, and when Mitch arrived I grabbed a book off the hall table, one I was never going to read, pulled on a jacket, and we were off.

The first thing I noticed was how polite he was opening the car door for me. I had forgotten he had always had such good manners. It kind of reminded me of Chris Hanson and prom night. I wondered what Chris was doing right at that moment, which kind of helped take the edge off my little heart attack when Mitch slid in on the driver's side and seemed to fill up every inch of space of the little VW. Not only was I sure he had gotten taller in Texas, but he must have added twenty pounds of muscle while he was away.

"Nice car," I said.

He laughed and rolled his eyes. "You're being kind. I know its old, but it gets me around and works, which is all I ask. My real love is my cycle."

My eyes widened. "You have a motorcycle?"

"Yep," he said, and flashed me a grin. "Think it could be fun riding on the back of one?"

"I think my dad would have a cow."

Secretly I thought *YES!* It would be a ton of fun and could picture myself in a black leather jacket, wild red curls flying in the breeze, and my arms wrapped tightly around his waist. But that was a fantasy that was way too sophisticated and crazy to share with anyone.

"Still like alternative?" he asked, bringing me back down to earth. I nodded, and while we were at a red light he grabbed a CD from the backseat and inserted it into the player. "It's a group from Austin," he said. I leaned back against the headrest and listened to one of the best bands I'd ever heard.

When we got to the library, I discovered that Mitch had reserved a conference room for us which meant he figured he needed some privacy for whatever he was going to say. As we took the stairs to the second floor, my heart rate started to accelerate and I didn't think it had anything to do with the climb.

We settled in across from each other at the small conference table. The table felt kind of symbolic, like all the stuff separating Mitch and me from the way we used to be. It made me feel a little sad.

He tossed his jacket onto an empty chair and leaned back in his chair giving me a measured look. "It's been a long time, Reds," he finally said. "Sometimes it seems a lot longer than a year. Now that I'm back, and since we have some of the same friends, I didn't want anything to be awkward for us. So I thought it would be good to kind of catch up. What do you think?"

I think I'd never include Emma Connors among our mutual friends. I didn't say that though. "Sure, that would be good," I said.

"You know I never wanted to leave Northfield, and I was pretty upset about my mom and dad splitting up." I nodded. "My mom and I fought constantly when I got down there. If it wasn't for basketball I'm not sure I would have stayed in school."

My mouth popped open. That was not what I expected to hear.

"I won't get into all of it, but I did some dumb things. Eventually I got my head on straight, and, when Dad got back from overseas and he was near retiring from the service, I had him promise that I could come back to New Jersey for my last two years of high school."

"I can't imagine being in a place you didn't want to be. I'm so ..." I started to reach out to touch his hand, but he quickly pulled it away.

"It's okay. I'm fine now. So what about you?" he said, trying to blow off the past like it was no big deal.

I shrugged. "Nothing much to tell. Hockey's turned out a lot better than last year. Played some lacrosse in the spring. It was fun. Jules and I did a bunch of hockey camps last summer. That's about it." I sounded like I was reciting a list, one that didn't include how much I had missed him and how glad he was back despite us not being together anymore.

He fiddled with his car keys that he had tossed on the table, sliding his fingers around the grooves on the keys. I could tell he was debating something. "So," he said at last, "you seeing anyone?" He didn't look up as he waited for my answer, just kept focusing on the keys.

I took a deep breath and slowly exhaled, trying to gather my thoughts. I hadn't expected him to ask, and wondered if he had meant Chris. "I haven't been seeing anyone," I said.

He raised his eyebrows as if he didn't believe me.

I started getting hot. "You know I've never lied to you."

He searched my face looking for deception and realized my words were true. "I'm sorry. Of course you don't. It's just I heard ..." Now it was his turn to be at a loss for words.

At least he knew the truth now and that made me feel better. I wanted to ask him about Emma, and why he couldn't see what a jerk she was, but didn't want to hear him defend her, so I started to stand, but he held up his hand like he had something more to say. "Hey, do you remember when you got your brother to bring you here freshmen year, and how he grilled me about my intentions with you?"

I couldn't help but giggle and then began to relax. "Yes, I remember," I said. "He was trying to protect me like he had done ever since I was a little kid." Then my thoughts got more serious. "But no one can protect a person from everything and it was hard when you left." *There, I said it. It's as close as I could come to telling him how much he mattered to me.*

Then I did stand up. "I think we've cleared the air, don't you?"

He picked up his jacket. I started for the door. "Reds," he said softly. "I'm sorry I left, too. Friends?" I turned to see his outstretched hand. Did I want to be friends? Heck no! I was still crazy about this boy, but to never speak, to have to avoid him? No, I didn't want that either.

I reached out my hand and felt his warm hand close around mine. The connection was instantaneous, like two magnets snapping together. *Had he sensed it, too?* I could feel the blood rushing to my face. Embarrassed by my obvious reaction, I quickly slipped my hand out of his and turned toward the door.

The ride home was pretty uneventful. We mostly talked about sports, a passion we still shared. His basketball season had just started and he was excited to be reunited with his old teammates. As he walked me to the door he said, "I'm flying back to Texas on Tuesday for Thanksgiving. Is it all right if I call you sometime when I get back? Maybe we can catch up some more, hit a movie, or something?"

I frowned. What would Emma think about that? "Uh, I don't know," I said. "You sure that'll be all right?" I was sure he knew I meant Emma.

Then it was his turn to frown. "Why wouldn't it be?" he said. If he was waiting for an answer from me he didn't get one. Finally he stepped back. "Tell your family I said hi, okay?"

I nodded. I watched him walk back to his car and drive away. I couldn't have imagined this day ever and wasn't sure what it all meant, but I had a game to think about and that had to be all that mattered.

(27)

It was so cool to return to school on Monday as Group Four Champions. Everywhere we went students and teachers were congratulating us, and still we weren't done. The state ran a Tournament of Champions that pitted the Group One Two, Three, and Four winners against each other, a 'best of the best' kind of thing. Some people thought we'd have the greatest chance of winning since we were the biggest school, but it wasn't necessarily so. Some of the smaller schools had great feeder programs just like Northfield did, and then the non-public schools got to recruit kids from out of their district and could have a ton of great players.

At lunch we were still keyed up over Saturday's game and I told Will about Mitch signaling me, and at first how I didn't understand what he meant about talking up a storm to the girl guarding me, and then when the light bulb went on, I finally got it.

"Maybe we wouldn't have won if it wasn't for Mitch," Sam said, half joking.

"Yeah," Anna said to me, with a twinkle in her eye, "Maybe you should tell him that."

Will snapped. "No, I'll tell him." There was an awkward silence, and then Will hunched forward over the table burying himself in his book. Noah thankfully started up on YouTube's latest music video and the moment passed.

At practice we found out we were being paired with the Group Two winner, and if we got past them, we'd face the winner of the Group One/Group Three game. Coach told us not to sweat the games as we were already state champions. When she said it that way, we all calmed down and thought the week ahead sounded pretty exciting. Then later on someone overheard Ms. Gillespie telling the goalies that Coach never had a team win it all, even though she had several state champion teams. Pretty soon everyone on the team knew it, and we were determined that we would do it for Coach.

After practice, Anna caught up with me as we walked to the locker room. "Sorry about Will today. He's normally such a cool-headed guy, but when it comes to Mitch he puts up a wall. I don't get it."

"Don't tell anyone, but Mitch and I met up yesterday." Anna's eyes nearly bugged out of her head. "He called it catching up." I rolled my eyes as I said this.

"I don't think Will knows about it," Anna said.

"If he did, something tells me he wouldn't be happy," I said.

Anna looked behind us making sure no one could overhear. "Did you and Will get along before Mitch left school?"

"Yeah. I got along with all his friends. After Mitch left, Kurt Evans even asked me out."

"You're kidding. What happened?"

"I told him no thanks. I don't think he was too happy, and then he really didn't speak to me after that."

We stopped by the locker room door to let some other players go by. Anna leaned against the brick wall thinking about our conversation. She snapped her fingers and started to pace back and forth. "And then you went to St. Benedict's prom with Chris Hanson, right?" she said, her voice rising in excitement. I nodded."Who here at Northfield knew you went with Chris?"

I started ticking off names. "Tori and Jules, of course, James, Noah, not too many. None of them would talk about it, though." Then I thought of someone else. "Emma Connors! She was at St. Benedict's prom."

"That's it," Anna said, stopping in her tracks. "Think about it. Emma tells her buddy, Kurt, she saw you at the prom. Kurt, who plays basketball with Will, wants to get even with you for rejecting him. Boom, that's how it gets all the way to Texas.

."But why would Will even bother telling Mitch?"

"I don't know. Maybe Mitch was missing you and Will wanted to help him get over you. What better way? You blew Mitch off and then turned around and went out with the biggest catch around. Most guys would have put you in the rearview mirror with that kind of news."

"But it wasn't like that," I said miserably.

"Will doesn't know that."Anna thought for a minute. "Maybe yesterday Mitch wanted to clear the air because he's forgiven you and has kind of moved on," she said.

"Yeah, with Emma Connors."

"Or," Anna's eyes brightened, "maybe Mitch is still crazy about you and wants to figure out if you would take him back."

I opened the locker room door and waved Anna through."You've got some mighty optimistic thinking going on there, Anna," I said to her retreating back. I heard her chuckle.

"You never know, Jackie. You never, know."

*   *   *

Tuesday was the last full day of school before Thanksgiving break and everyone was anxious for the vacation to start. Teachers were snapping on everyone, even the good students, trying to keep us working hard. I figured maybe they needed time away from us more than we did from them. When I got home from practice I surfed through my email to find a few more congratulations from college coaches. And then I spotted an email that made me break out in a grin.

It was from Chris Hanson wishing me luck in the next day's game. He wrote all about his school and his crazy roommate who was not a jock at all, but someone who wrote poetry and spent most of his days sitting on the floor playing some strange musical instrument from India. He had me laughing with each paragraph he wrote, and as I shut down my computer, I wondered how he could find school such an exciting place to be while I still found the whole idea of college such an uncomfortable one.

*   *   *

The day of our next game felt more like summer than the tail end of November. Even if it hadn't been a game day it still would have been hard to sit in class and not wish we were anywhere else besides school. When we got out at noontime to start the Thanksgiving vacation, it felt like the whole school was breaking out of jail. The bus ride was an hour of endless chatter and joking around. As I looked around, it seemed like we had become one enormous family.

Even the sophomores, who mostly played JV, had caught up in the excitement of how much we had achieved.

We were facing a team from Central Jersey who had won their group championship five out of the last six years, which had to be some kind of record. Jules told me their coach was as well known in the state as Mrs. Fortunata, and I wondered how they felt finally facing off against one another.

After our warmup, we huddled together for Coach to give us our final instructions. "Girls, I'm so proud of everything you've accomplished this season. I don't want it to end. Do you?"

We all screamed, "NO!" and I could feel the energy coming off each one of us building and building. We were going to get them.

We raced onto the field, adrenaline pumping through our veins. The next hour flew by so fast I can't even remember the details, only that we won. People said we played great, that they'd never seen such good hockey from a high school team. Maybe they were right. I don't know. All I remember thinking as we walked off the field was just one more game to go.

After the game Dad signaled me to join him at the roped off area that surrounded the field. "There's someone I want you to meet," he said. I slipped under the rope and Dad and I walked over to a tall middle-aged woman with short sandy hair that was just starting to turn gray. "Jackie, this is Nancy Wright," Dad said.

The lady's deep blue eyes sparkled as she shook my hand. "Congratulations. Wonderful game, Jackie."

I thanked her, then didn't know what else to say, but she saved me when she said, "I really can't say anything more, NCAA rules you know, but I hope some time you'll visit our school."Then she stepped away, nodded to my Dad, and walked off toward the parking lot.

Dad patted my hand. "We spoke for awhile, honey. She seemed to be impressed. Maybe sometime we'll take a ride out there. If you want to that is."

Did I want to? Maybe, but there was still one more game to go.

I thought Mitch might call and ask about the game, but he didn't. Each night before Sunday's final game I would glance over to my phone, flip it open to make sure it was on and charged, just in case. With each disappointment, I had to remind myself that he said something about calling after he got back. I was taking our 'renewed friendship' a lot more serious than I should have.

On Saturday we had a team get-together at the Hansons. Coach sat us down to talk about the final game. She read us some messages from alumnae, some from many years past wishing us well on our school's first try at winning the Tournament of Champions. There was one from Mandy Stevenson saying she wished she could be there, but had to be back at college earlier in the day. "My parents will be there, though, and they'll be giving me a play-by-play. I'm so excited for you guys." Listening to her message made me feel like she was right back on the field with us, like an extra weapon.

I couldn't figure out which had my team more excited, hearing those messages, or being able to feast their eyes on Chris Hanson who had returned home from college for Thanksgiving.

As he circulated around the room, making sure everyone had all the food they needed, the girls couldn't seem to take their eyes off him. Mr. Hanson was about bursting with pride that his daughters were playing for such high stakes and I was wondering if Mrs. Hanson would give him a get-out-of-jail card and let him see the game. He hadn't been to one since his flare up with Tori.

Chris and I had a few minutes to talk before the party broke up. He wished me luck, and said he was driving back right after the game, so probably wouldn't see me for awhile. I asked him if he had broken many hearts yet, and he laughed saying he didn't know since he only had eyes for me. Most girls would have melted on that one, but I knew he was a teaser. Not for the first time was I relieved I had put a 'do-not-trespass' sign over my heart in elementary school when it came to Chris 'cause he was just about perfect.

*   *   *

Sunday morning I could feel my family giving me secret looks during breakfast. "What?" I said to my dad, who was trying to be nonchalant, peeping over the sports page at me.

"Just wondering how you were feeling," he said.

My mom was busy making pancakes, but even she, the biggest non-sports fan in the universe, except when it came to my brother, was nervous. She had already dropped some egg shells into the mixing bowl, and then had to re-clean the skillet when she burned the first batch of pancakes.

"It's just another game," I exclaimed. But it wasn't, and I hurried to the bathroom for the hundredth time that morning.

An hour later my dad dropped me and the twins off at school. Tori had been unusually quiet on the ride, and Jules had snapped at her sister more than once for no reason at all. Finally Jules turned her attention to me. "You have everything, right?" she muttered like I was some idiot that couldn't remember stuff for such a big game.

"Yes," I answered back. Frankly I wanted to bite Jules' head off, but held my tongue for the good of the team.

Once we were all seated on the bus, Ms. Gillespie counted heads to make sure we were all there, and then we were off. As we hit the entrance to the turnpike I could sense something was off. Our usual jovial, boisterous team had gone missing.

When we were on the field, Jules and Kate were trying to pump up the team as we went through our warmup, but their words had a hollow sound like they really didn't believe what they were saying. I looked around at my teammates, then checked out our opponents, Mystic Highlands, taking corners at the other end of the field. A cold wind whipped across my face, another reminder that hockey was almost over and it would soon be winter's turn to rule. I wondered if the other team was feeling it, too.

In the opening minutes I knew we were in trouble. We sure weren't acting like the powerhouse that had won the semi-finals with our constant turnovers and missed connections. Had we been beamed up by extra-terrestrials? It was the only thing that made sense. I sent a crisp pass to Sam. All she had to do was touch it with her stick and the ball would have deflected into the cage. It was something we had practiced over and over all season. She muffed it entirely and we both watched the ball trickle out-of-bounds. "Sorry," she said, and shook her head not quite believing she had missed such an easy goal.

"'Sokay," I said, "we'll get the next one." But we didn't, and the time dragged on.

By halftime we seemed like lost travelers whose GPS had run out of juice. Then Sam ran over to the bench and fished into her stick bag for something. When she came back she asked Coach if she could speak to the team herself. Coach was pretty darn smart, and knew when it was time for a team to sort things out for themselves, so she walked over to the bench.

Then Sam opened up her hand. She was holding a small piece of rope roughly cut at both ends. I stared at it, and then at Sam. "It's the rope!" I exclaimed.

She nodded and grinned. "Guys, it's the rope from freshman year," she said. Then we all took turns telling the younger players, about how our class had been hazed by the upperclassmen, and were tied up in the woods and left there, and how it was Sam's penknife that had gotten us out.

"That was a tough night," Anna said, shaking her head at the memory.

"We became a team that night. We needed everyone or we'd have never gotten home," Jules said.

"You guys can never tell anyone about it, okay?" Sam said. "Not even Coach."

"Let's give a cheer for the rope," Lindsay said. We were cracking up by now, and as we put our hands together, half laughing, we cheered out the word "rope."

As we jogged back onto the field our mood felt tons lighter. Sam had just reminded us how tough we really were when we stuck together, and it began to show as soon as the ref blew her whistle. As the clock ticked down, more and more opportunities were coming our way and I was sure something good would happen. It was only a matter of time.

With less than a minute left Jules sent me a killer pass that let me cut off the last defender. There was just me and the goalie left. I did my little stutter step figuring it was a piece of cake, but I must have given something away. The goalie read me perfectly, and as she went down to the ground to block me she was able to clear the ball away with her stick. The whistle blew. Game over.

I couldn't believe it. We were going into overtime and it was all my fault. As we went to the sidelines there were tears in my eyes. Then I felt someone pat me on the back. It was Tori. "Remember the easiest ones are the toughest?" she said. I thought back to our conversation on the tennis court. She was right. How could I give advice to someone and not take the same advice myself? I lifted the hem of my shirt and dried my eyes. We were going to win this thing.

The overtime tiebreaker was putting seven of our best players against seven of theirs. Usually somebody scores and somebody did. It wasn't me, the one the team usually counted on. It was the new kid, Cassie Henry. She finally could use her blazing speed in the now wide open field and slammed the ball past the goalie.

As the final whistle blew everyone piled on top of her, including me. What a feeling! We were all squished together, the clean unproven ones from the bench, and the dirty smelly ones from the field, and we were all the same. We were all one.

After we received the trophy, one that was a lot heavier than I had ever imagined, our families came onto the field to take the customary pictures. A reporter was talking to Coach and Cassie, and then she came over to me. She stuck the microphone inches from my face and said, "Cassie Henry said she would have never been on the team if it hadn't been for you helping her out. Can you comment?"

I looked at her for a long minute wondering where reporters come up with some of their questions. I glanced at Coach who was standing a few yards away watching me. I smiled at the reporter and said, "Helping Cassie made me realize how much I want to be a coach someday."I thought it was a good answer and hoped the reporter would go away. She didn't.

"How bad did you feel about missing that goal in the closing minutes of regulation?"

I looked at her in disbelief. How did she think I felt?I paused for a few seconds to gather my thoughts, and then I said, "Sometimes the easiest goals get away from you and sometimes you just have to get over it and get on with the game." She knew I didn't really answer her question. But it was all she was going to get from me. As I walked away to join my teammates I have to say that handling that reporter was a bit of an extra victory for me on this best of days.

(28)

Returning to school Monday, after winning the Tournament of Champions the day before, was sure a big letdown. Yesterday everyone had wanted my picture and to hear what I had to say. Now kids were going through the hallways like it was any old day and I felt as anonymous as all the other two thousand or more kids at our school. It was almost like being crowned the number one team in the state never happened.

I spun the dial on my lock, and then, as I opened my locker, a familiar sight, a piece of paper floated toward the floor. As I snagged it out of the air, I read —

Congratulations – you're number one with me, too!

It made me smile. Now I knew the writer for sure. It had to be Cassie, and this latest note was her way of thanking me again for helping her out at the start of the season.

"Hey," I wanted to yell at the top of my lungs as kids passed by, "we're the top team in the whole state!" Sitting in homeroom, I patiently waited for the congratulations that would come after morning announcements. When the intercom came on, I began tapping my foot. *They must be saving the best for last,* I thought as they went through the list — Spanish Club meeting canceled, reminder to get permission slips in for the trip to Washington, tickets for the winter dance will go on sale Friday, etc. The announcer was ending the list when she said, "Oh, by the way, the field hockey team won the Tournament of Champions yesterday."

That's it? That's it? What planet does this girl live on? To be fair, a few kids turned in their seats and offered their congratulations, but I could tell from the general lack of excitement they were just being polite.

As soon as I got to gym, Anna and Sam came over to my locker. "It feels kind of weird with nothing to do this afternoon," Anna said, as she sat down next to me. "I'm kind of bummed."

"Not me. I've still got a buzz on," Sam said, as she finished tying her sneakers.

"I'm not even sure many kids even care what we did," I said, slamming the locker and snapping the lock shut.

"Why should they?" Sam said, as we started to walk to the gym. She saw the surprised look on my face. "Jack, everybody's got their own thing. Ours is hockey. That's all."

I followed her out to the gym. "But what we did was a big deal, right?" I said.

"Hugh," Sam answered. "But to us, Jackie, only to us."

Anna, who was a step or two behind us, grabbed my hand and said, "Change of subject." She waited until she had our attention. "Will's asked me to the winter dance," and she busted a dance move around Sam and me that had both of us laughing.

"That's great," I said. I was really happy for her 'cause I knew how much she liked him.

Then Sam raised an eyebrow and looked at me. "Wallflower," I said, laughing, and we both high-fived our predicament. We might not be going to a dance, but at least we had a trophy.

When I got home that day there was a note from Mom saying she and Dad had gone with Lizzie and taken Grandma back to the shore, and I could start moving my things back into my room. I skipped the stairs two at a time. I'd miss Grandma, but I was glad to get my old room back. I smelled the hint of lemon polish immediately, and noticed the room was a lot neater than when I left it. *Thank you, Grandma!* Sitting on my desk was one of those "You Did It" cards. On the inside Grandma thanked me for lending her my room, and then she added, "I can't wait to tell the girls at bridge, and all those youngsters in my yoga class that I have a granddaughter whose team is number one." I took the note and put it in the top drawer of my desk. I was going to it save it forever.

Tori called me later that night. "Guess what? Jake Solazzo asked me to the winter dance."

"Who's he?" I said, wondering how the heck Tori found so many new guys.

"Only the captain of the basketball team," she said. "I finally got one taller than me, and he's a senior, too."

"Wow Tori, a team captain and a senior. Double the fun!" Tori laughed and went on about how she was going to be able to wear high heels. The next five minutes were a one-sided discussion on what she should look for in a dress.

"It's not formal is it?" I said, trying to show some interest. I hadn't really thought about the dance. When Mitch and I were together the dance got snowed out, and then last year, I kind of tuned out the normal school stuff after Mitch left.

"No. It's a notch up from everyday, but definitely nothing fancy," Tori said.

As Tori was further describing dress possibilities I tuned her out. *First Will, and now the team captain. Is the whole basketball team going?* I pictured Mitch with Emma, her arms wrapped around him, and made a face. I was glad no one had asked me to the dance. It would have been horrible to have to watch them together like that.

I came out of my musings when Tori said, "Sorry I couldn't help you out about Mitch. No one seems to know the deal. I do know that Emma does not have a date yet. I overheard someone ask her what she was wearing, and she said she wasn't sure she was going to bother with the dance."

"Mitch has been in Texas."

"Well, I guess that explains it. Probably didn't have time to ask her yet."

The next day I opened my locker and found another note. It was so unexpected that before I could grab it, it fluttered to the floor. I watched in horror as it was kicked about, and quickly pushed my way out into the middle of the hallway yelling, "Look out, look out," as I reached down and snatched it up before it was torn to shreds.

When I opened it I was shocked. It read —

Since you put everything on the line and won a state title, I'm hoping you'll take another chance. This time, with me. Let's meet after school at your locker. I have something to ask you.

I looked around to see if anyone was trying to gauge my reaction, but everyone was moving along, minding their own business. I hurried to homeroom and slid into my seat. My heart was pounding, and my mind was puzzling over the note. I knew the writer wasn't anyone from the team anymore. I chewed on my pen trying to figure out what to do. Someone had my back all this season. Could I deny the writer a date just because I didn't want to see Mitch there with Emma?

I talked it over with Anna and Sam in gym. "It sounds so romantic and mysterious," Anna said.

Sam frowned. "It could be some stalker dude. Maybe you should just take off after school."

I put my friends' advice inside my already crowded brain and decided the final person to ask was James. As I took my seat in English, I considered the possibility that the writer might actually be James. He wasn't attached anymore and we always got along. *Could it be?* I studied him out of the corner of my eye. He didn't look like he was holding onto a secret. Could he really want to be with me after Jules? That would be too weird. Still ...

"What are you doing after school today?" I asked toward the end of class. I think my question kind of surprised him, and then he grinned.

"Why? You got something in mind?" he asked, raising his eyebrow and giving me a flirty grin.

I gulped. I didn't know what to say ... "no" and hurt his feelings or "yes" and be stuck with the consequences. The bell rang, and coward that I was, I stood up and said, "See you later."

I took my time going to my locker. I was almost afraid to see who would show up. Maybe it would be some strange guy I didn't know, or maybe it would be James and he had been just teasing me in class. I stopped in the lavatory, and then postponed the inevitable even further by giving my dry mouth a little relief at the water fountain.

I spun my lock looking over my shoulder occasionally to see if anyone was coming toward my locker, but the hallway was still crowded. I slammed my locker shut and leaned against the wall and waited.

Then I saw a tall dark-haired boy blocked by some other boys. The other boys stopped at another locker and Mitch Kennedy came walking toward me. *Maybe he's going to congratulate me for the state title.* I gave him a tentative smile.

"Congratulations, Reds. You must feel like you're on top of the world."

So that's what he wanted to say. Of course.

I took in how good he looked in his gray V-neck sweater and black jeans, and sighed. I had been such a lucky girl back then.

We stared into each other's eyes, and it seemed for a moment like we were the only ones in the building. Then Mitch broke the spell as he reached into his back pockets and pulled out two pieces of paper, and held them up to me, one in each hand. There was a '**YES**' and a '**NO**' printed in the same distinctive type as all my notes. He stepped closer. "Two years ago we were supposed to go together to the winter dance but it got canceled with the snowstorm. It's been a long time and I've thought about you a lot. Will you give me a second chance and go with me now?"

My mind reeled. Mitch had sent me all those notes, almost since the time he had returned to Northfield. And it was he who was asking me to the dance. I thought back to my birthday wishes — a state championship and Mitch Kennedy back in the halls of Northfield High. Not too much to ask for when you turn sixteen, right?

I could feel my face growing warm as he patiently waited for my answer. As I reached for the '**YES**' I saw his face light up. I slipped the paper into my back pocket."Yes," I whispered. "The answer is definitely yes."

Epilogue

Every story should have a "definitely yes" ending. And mine was a perfect moment for sure, but life didn't stop there. To begin with there was saying goodbye to hockey, at least for awhile, Even handing back my uniform was a sad moment. Having to turn in my number two shirt and kilt was like having to empty out a closet full of my favorite clothes. And I wondered briefly, what my next season would be like when I wore Northfield's blue and white shirt for the final time.

We did have a huge victory party thrown by the Hansons with all of the parents helping out. We ate like we had been stranded on a desert island for days with only rainwater and plant leaves to survive. As we sat on their rec room floor and stuffed ourselves, it came to me that a lot of my teammates would soon be fading out of my everyday life. Those of us who had after school jobs might go for weeks without seeing one another. I would especially miss Sam who worked all the time when she wasn't playing hockey. Then again, I had promised my boss at the movie theater I could be counted on to work every Saturday and most Sundays so I was going to be busy, too.

I was beyond happy that Mitch and I found our way back to each other. It might not have happened if he hadn't taken his time and slowly eased his way back into my life.

We discovered we had both changed a lot since freshmen year, but our mutual attraction was stronger than ever.

It wasn't always easy for us to find the time to be together, but we were determined to make it work. Mitch's basketball season was in full swing, and it turned out basketball wasn't the only thing taking up his time. "It's not really a job," he said one night when we were down in my basement shooting pool. "It's a service project where I'll be working on Sundays in the city of Camden. Congressman Anders has organized it."

"How come you're working for him?" I asked as I took a bead on a striped ball sitting in the far corner.

"I'm trying to get his recommendation for the Air Force Academy," he said.

I blinked at the news, and missed my shot entirely. College was tapping on everyone's door, and we weren't halfway through junior year. I was feeling a lot of pressure, too. Some colleges wanted me to come see their schools and commit to them right away, but I wasn't ready.

I had gone to Coach about it shortly before I took the dreaded SATs. "Suppose I do awful on Saturday," I said.

"If you do, you can still take them again," she said, as she swung her chair from side to side. "Jackie, many coaches can help you get in if they really want you, but admissions offices will look at your grades, too. The most important thing is to do your best in your school work so you're truly prepared for college."

She paused a moment to pick up the picture of her two sons that always sat on her desk, and studied it for a moment. "I want you to know," she said, as she replaced the picture, "that no matter what, I will help you with your college choice." Then before I left her office she reminded me of a team meeting she wanted to have with us the following week.

I figured the meeting was going to be about next summer's camps and was wondering where she would suggest we go. But that was not what the afternoon was about, not at all. When we piled into the health room it was like we hadn't seen each other in a year, and not the three weeks since the season ended. Gossip and catching up was exploding through the air.

Finally Coach arrived and the room quieted down. "Thank you all for coming," she said, as she leaned against the desk in the front of the room. "First of all I'd like to thank each and every one of you for a season I will never forget. I'm more proud of you than I can ever say. I wish those of you who are returning a season that equals this one in every way."

Something about what she was saying didn't sound right. I sat up a little straighter and looked over at Jules. She was frowning, so she must have felt something was a little off, too.

Coach cleared her throat and went on. "Normally this would be a meeting about camps, but that will be for another time. There will be an article in tomorrow's newspaper, and I wanted to meet with all of you before you saw it," she said.

Now I was on high alert. You could hear a pin drop in the room. Something big was happening and everyone knew it.

"The company my husband works for has been bought out by another company," Coach said. "He's being transferred next month to offices in Boston. Our sons and I will be joining him shortly after that."

Suddenly the room was buzzing. "Coach was going to Boston? What about next season? When would she be back?"

Finally Jules spoke up. "Coach, is this permanent? You're leaving for good?"

Coach gave Jules a small smile. "Yes. I'll be resigning from Northfield in a few weeks. Girls, I'll miss you all like crazy, but I know whoever they hire as the next coach will be a good one, and will carry on Northfield's great tradition."

I don't care how good the person will be. It isn't you Coach. I felt the tears forming in my eyes, and tried to think of happier things like going to the dentist or taking the SATs everyday for a week.

I was barely listening as Coach said, "... and because of this I've decided to name next year's captains now so leadership is in place to help the new coach." *Jules would be good I thought, probably as good as Mandy Stevenson, but what did it matter without Coach?*

"Your captains for next year will be Jules Hanson and Jackie McKendry."

There was a burst of applause. Then Jules stood up, and came over and gave me a hug. I heard Cassie, who was sitting behind me, lean into my ear and say, "I'm so glad it's you. You sure deserve it."

I smiled and said thanks because it was what was expected, but the real me had already run away hiding in some dark cave knowing that Mrs. Fortunata would no longer be in my life. She was my role model, the person who had inspired me to want to be a coach myself. I would be lost without her.

After the meeting, when most of my teammates had left the room to go their separate ways, Coach pulled Jules and me aside. "I know this news was a surprise, but I had to tell you now before you heard it from someone else. You'll make wonderful captains together. I couldn't leave this team in better hands." She looked at both of us. "I'm counting on you girls to help the new coach, and the team will take its cue from how you handle things."

"We'll do it, Coach," Jules said with confidence.

"I'll try my best," I said my eyes beginning to fill again, already dreading the thoughts of senior year.

Then Coach gave me a hug and said, "I know you will, Jackie McKendry. You always do."

The End

Acknowledgements

I'd like to thank the countless people who helped me tweak this story over the last two years, especially Diane Birkbeck, Jen McGill, Tricia Scrivani, and Carling Mott. A major thank you goes to my editing buddy, Sarah Keller, who surprisingly was willing to put up with my countless grammatical errors once again. Special hugs and kisses go to my grandson, Connor McGill, who was so cooperative in taking long naps, as I madly typed at his mother's dining room table for much of the story's initial draft. My wish for him is that he might meet a little Jackie McKendry of his own someday.

CPSIA information can be obtained at www.ICGtesting.com
Printed in the USA
BVOW03s0115291014

372718BV00008B/133/P